MINNESOTA STORIES

Kirk House Publishers

Dedicated to Colleen Szot

Colleen, this is for you.
You always saw the best in all of us and
for years wanted to put our work in
a collection. We finally did it!

MINNESOTA STORIES

A Collection of 28 Fiction
Stories About the
State We Love

Compiled by Women of Words

First Edition
978-1-952976-74-2 paperback
978-1-952976-75-9 eBook
978-1-952976-76-6 hardcover
Library of Congress Control Number: 2022910502

Cover and Interior Design by Ann Aubitz

Published by Kirk House Publishers
1250 E 115th Street
Burnsville, MN 55337
Kirkhousepublishers.com
612-781-2815

If you want to contact Women of Words please go to our website contact page. https://www.womenofwordsconference.com

Table of Contents

Introduction

In 1994, five women met around a kitchen table, talking about writing over lunch. They were writing books about business, poetry, their lives, or their passions.

These women became friends and had strong support for each other. Then one asked if she could bring a writer friend to the group—and so did others. By 1997, this small but growing group decided to move its lunch meeting to a restaurant to allow for more visitors. Each visitor brought new life and a new story. Those who cherished the group felt a strong connection and started sharing. Soon you could see the kinship reverberate throughout this new sisterhood.

Such was the modest beginning of our writer's group that eventually became WOW–Women of Words. "Wow" is what we often shout when we hear a great story or a good idea. At monthly meetings, WOW women willingly share their victories—and just as readily share their mistakes, with the belief that we help each other most with our honesty.

Sometimes when we are being funny, we'll say that WOW's motto is: Tell us what you did right so we can do it too, and tell us what you did wrong, so we don't do it. And today, it's all about being helpful and supportive—just like it started almost 30 years ago.

This collection of 28 stories is as unique as are the members, and each brings a different part of life to our eyes—some funny, some poignant, some very thoughtful, but all worth your time. The idea of a collection has been dancing around for years, but it took a member who recently said, "The WOW women should have a book," to make it happen. The rest, as they say, is now history held in your hands.

Special women, long-term friendships, and a long, long list of books now published—and many women with a smile and satisfactory feeling of success, completion, and fulfilling her dream. *That's what we help each other do.*

We believe that "once a writer, always a writer," and our members have proven that.

~Connie Anderson, Co-Founder of Women of Words

STORY 1
Anointing
MARY KAY CRAWFORD

❖

I take consecutive pictures of you, seated in your wheelchair beneath a crabapple tree, hoping for that best shot—you with both eyes open and the sort of smile on your face when you sing along with Lawrence Welk on Saturday night, Dad seated beside you.

Today, dear Mom, you are the queen of Elliott Park.

The longest-reigning, longest-lived in the park across the street from your nursing home residence.

Just days shy of your 89th birthday.

The wind lifts tickled-pink and pale-pink clustered blossoms gently above your head as an anointing of this moment.

You look heavenward with eyes of wonder.

In a state of ease and lightness.

"Life is a miracle," you say.

Your story starts backward from kindergarten.

"I clearly remember being in kindergarten with our beautiful teacher, Ms. Bennett. That's when I decided to become a teacher," you tell me.

You remember happy summers with your grandma and grandpa on their northern Minnesota farm. Picking blueberries, jumping into piles of hay stored in the barn, watching your grandpa round up a herd of cattle with the assistance of his majestic full-coated Collie barking at their heels. Bossy, the cow always in the lead, a cowbell jangling around her neck. At day's end, you say, how you and Grandma and Grandpa sat at the end of a sandy road leading to their rustic farmhouse and watched the sun go down.

"Life—it's all a miracle," you sigh.

You lift an unsteady arm, weakened by prolonged years of arthritis, and wave at the camera.

Your well-loved peach-colored cardigan hangs loose and ragged at your wrist.

You refuse to wear the new cardigans I've placed in your closet. The last time I brought your peach-colored cardigan to the dry cleaners they pinned a disclaimer to it stating: *"There's not much more we can do with this sweater."*

Is this a wave goodbye? Are you taking leave of this earth, I wonder, wearing your Raggedy Ann peach-colored cardigan?

Or is this goodbye to a calamitous year of strife in our cities and the Covid pandemic that both you and Dad SURVIVED?

The sun has moved into your eyes, and you squint in the glow of early afternoon light.

Awash in direct sunlight, your frail visage pales against the fragrance of this moment, captured in full spring bloom of bold floral blossoms, the vibrant green of grass and treetops.

You seem to be disappearing into the cushions of your wheelchair, becoming more spirit than body, more heaven than earth.

The wind pauses for breath, then moves past you and through the leaves with a whisper.

———•———

Life is not meant to rob us of everything we cherish, I've heard.

So, what will you take with you? Memories of this moment? Memories of the children you raised, your husband, your carefree childhood, your days as a fifth-grade schoolteacher?

What memories will you leave me? My mind's eye wanders to the deep reddish-brown mahogany box holding Grandma's sterling silver flatware.

Clean silver when first placed into container, the silver plaque fastened to the inside lid reads.

This container is specially treated to keep silver placed in it from tarnishing.

The silver still gleaming and polished as the day Grandma laid it out with her rose-patterned china, the year before she passed.

Your mother, my mother—instructed to keep the container lid closed at all times to prevent tarnishing.

Suddenly, I feel nostalgic for Grandma's midcentury home with dark wood cabinets, the built-in breakfront crowded with unevenly stacked china, behind glass doors with black metal closures that clicked and creaked as doors adjusted to open and close. My sister and I would carefully remove our doll-sized white coffee cups that Grandma would then fill with more milk than coffee to dunk our white sugar cubes. Eventually, more sugar than milk.

<hr>

But now, in Elliott Park, my mom's image is fading, her memory wanes. She argues with me and forgets what she wanted to say.

Amazingly, she remembers the words to Lawrence Welk's Good Night song. I hear the "Goodnight" and the "Au Revoir" and the talk of sweet sorrow. She sings to Elliott Park from the comfort of her wheelchair as the park hums along in birdsong and wind rustles through the leaves.

What miracles and wonders will I remember a year from now? Two years from now?

When I'm an old woman, will I return to this very place in Elliott Park covered in a canopy of flowering trees and feel the anointing of this moment, my mother's spirit in the flowering clusters of apple blossoms and long, outstretched branches?

Or will I lift the lid in a moment of breathtaking stillness and peek inside the mahogany box lined with rose-colored velvet at the quietly placed silverware, still polished and beautiful as the day your mother gave it to you? The day you left it to me.

 Mary Kay Crawford-Lorfink has been published in *WINK: Writers in the Know* magazine, *Creatopia* magazine and Amazon books, graduated with a BA in English from the U of MN, is an on-going student at The Loft Literary Center, Minneapolis, MN, and a member of WOW - Women of Words. "Writing is a mystical experience—turning wonder into story."

Behind the Reflection

LISA CARMICHAEL

If Elise had to listen to one more problem of the members of this congregation she would be on the road to insanity, which was a chapter of someone else's story. Not hers. Not a minister's wife. The years in Ridgely township had been long and tiresome.

Her faith was all she had, but all these problems battered her. Just like the church bell moving back and forth every 30 minutes, reminding her of time wasted; she was failing at life. This failing feeling brought words into her head that would frighten and surprise her husband. The curse words would surface in her mind each time the bell tapped side to side.

Where was this coming from? It's a question she often asked herself, this perfect-looking, seemingly happy woman who others looked up to and admired. Yet, behind her sparkling, welcoming exterior was a much darker reality. This young woman was anything but perfect. She's troubled, she's damaged, and desperately trying to keep it all together, but ultimately, not doing a very good job. Her life was a mess, filled with exhausting thoughts, and she worried how much time before it would come crashing down. What else could explain why she would be so comfortable living in such an isolated, cold climate in southern Minnesota? How could she be messed up on the inside? Yes, appearances can be deceiving, but was there something more?

Looking at herself in the mirror, Elise didn't see the glorified housecleaner and nanny she had become. She didn't know whose eyes were staring back at her. No matter what direction she turned, she wondered who this was looking intensely back at her. There was a chapter of another life behind the glare. Was her own life just one chapter in a much larger story?

Time seemed to stop; the look deepened with every micro-second. The curiosity deepened. She was on red alert. Her heart raced as she kept replaying this story of another life while she looked in the mirror. How could a minister's wife have memories of a past life, she asked herself.

Her gaze allowed the chemicals in her body to stop time for the next twenty seconds which seemed to be a lifetime of someone else.

Elise had grown up in Nicollet County. She'd lived through the rough weather year after year. Nothing an old sweater couldn't solve, but this was a strange feeling—she knew it wasn't the fierce winter blizzard that had just rolled in that was creating this mixture of strangeness.

She was a woman, a mother, who others looked up to and admired. And yet, here she was playing the martyr—a fake. It was all an act, a facade she had created to hide her own insecurity and self-doubt. It was tiresome, this constant charade. Was she even playing the role right?

What she saw in the mirror was not the reflection of what everyone wanted her to be. This naive nature of hers couldn't believe what she was seeing.

Her mind was racing like a single bicycle tire rolling down a steep hill that keeps spinning and spinning downward as she runs after it. The bicycle tire never stops rolling downward. This life was to be the answer, but instead it only brought more hopelessness. All these annoying problems cast on her like spells from those who wanted to be her friend and confidant.

Elise hated this arrangement. It was just a twenty second look into the old antique stained mirror. The crack on the side reminded her of the years of brokenness that were looking back at her. As she looked deeply into the dark eyes in the mirror, the uncertainty comforted her. It made her feel important and justified. These racing thoughts were not logical; still they were pulling her in deeper.

No one knew this side of her. She was the opposite of calmness. The perfect dream was now a nightmare. She was unstable, complex, and full of curiosity, probing deeper with every second.

She opened her mouth, gasping, noticing the flush, the redness in her skin from the salty tears that were rolling down her cheeks and irritating her skin. This was all so wrong. Water was meant for play, not for sadness. Looking deep, she wondered, where was the woman who might be dancing on the beach splashing the salty waves? Her redness only reminded her more of what she didn't have.

She often wondered if she was meant to be somewhere else. Each time she looked into that round mirror she was reminded of something distant, of the truth that she desperately wanted to understand. A minister's wife is not what it seems–holding so many secrets and burdens. She never had the time or the desire, to look in the mirror. She had no desire because it frightened her.

This brief look in the mirror today triggered frustration. It reminded her there was nothing to look forward to, just all the work that needed attention. The busyness never ended. She had no time to look forward because this was her life now.

Today was different. This moment was different. There was someone inside the mirror. Had this happened before? Was there a life that lived behind that gaze as she tried to focus again? She didn't understand what she was imagining. Had she seen this person before? As she looked into her own eyes, was she being transformed by this person from a different world?

The look she saw was breaking her heart. Elise knew she must be living her life in someone else's body. Her life was not meant to be like this. The overwhelm and anxiousness was a nervous breakdown in the making. And she couldn't run away. She was fulfilling a grim sentence that wasn't for her. Who was looking back at her? What was her truth? She wanted to morph into the mirror. She fantasized that the mirror could solve everything for her.

The country church bell rang in the background. The clanging sound was begging her to come to reality, but the face she saw was desperately needing her, today, now. She needed to look away, but was pulled deeper into the person watching her. The same needful look that came from everyone else and all the problems that needed her attention. Tasks called her too.

The cooking, the cleaning, and the laundry, always begging, never done. How long could it all wait? None of this gave her the sense of security she assumed life would bring her. It made her feel hopeless without feeling that it mattered. All the work waiting for her pushed her deeper into the reflection, looking for the life of someone else. Now as she looked, there was someone she recognized. Bravely leaning forward, she wanted the truth. She didn't have much time.

The isolation from the snowstorm was difficult for everyone. It snowed and blew snow for three days. The temperature kept dropping. No one could leave the house. It was horrible for her own children. Fight after fight, and the relentless complaining was irritating. There wasn't much food. Everyone was cold. She was sure the next day she would lose all feeling in her toes. Someone was always crying. Edward had gotten over a cold. Mary didn't look good and hadn't kept food in her stomach in days. She looked like she was losing weight again. Why were these terrible things happening to her children?

The neighbor was only trying to help by bringing them food, but he brought his worries too, not realizing his struggles were burdensome to hear. It was terribly sad to hear about how weak and frail his parents were. They needed to be in the hospital, but there was nothing she could do. She was ordered to stay inside.

Looking into the mirror, more tears came to her eyes. Everything was so sad because there was nothing she could do. She understood her neighbor's pain. It had to have been horrible living in these conditions while watching his parents' lives slowly slip away.

She remembered their smiles through their crooked and broken teeth, telling stories of their hard work and monotonous lives. Now so frail, it was upsetting that their lives had been ridiculously difficult. He was the only surviving son of their five children. The pain she felt for them ran through her body, through her heart, and made her mind race faster. His short visit was disturbing. Grieving his loss consumed her. She herself would never see them again. It was a heartbreaking feeling she had felt before.

With a sigh, she looked closer into the mirror, and saw only the look of fear that dried the tears. Her heart pounded faster and faster. The woman in the mirror understood but looked hopeless as well.

She couldn't smile back. Elise saw the stare only her grandma wore. Why now? Why did Grandmother have to appear? She had no soul. She was evil. She was a mole, a miser, and somewhat of a thief. She pathetically saved every breadcrumb and forced her bad habits onto her grandchildren. She was angry after Elise's mother passed away that she was stuck caring for her granddaughter. She was a miserable old woman and didn't have time for anyone. Despite everything, Elise wanted to be like her, but finally gave up trying.

She gave up trying when she realized how terrible a human being her grandmother was. No one wanted to be around her. No one could please her. No one could make her happy. When Elise told her grandmother she was marrying John, the response was sarcasm and disappointment. She didn't understand. Wasn't this the biggest favor she could do for her grandma?

Instead, Grandmother cursed me and cursed my marriage. Why now? Why was this evil woman staring back now? She ignored our birthdays and was much happier living life alone. She was hateful. More sadness crept inside

Elise thinking of the loneliness of her life. *Was I becoming her? Was I her? Was this why I was seeing her reflection?*

Looking deeper into those sad deep withdrawn eyes was an introvert who was afraid of her own smile. The sadness she saw was overwhelming. Her messy bun was an attempt at making life easier by pulling the messy curls together.

Bringing her hair together never worked though. Wishing for the perfected bun her grandmother once wore wasn't worthy of comparison. It was a comparison only because their hair color was the same.

The pain of her childhood stared back at her each time she looked at her hair shaped into a bun. It was frustrating to see that pulling her hair tightly back only made the frown and worry lines easier for everyone to see. No one understood these deep lines that scarred her. Looking closely, it was as if she had lived this moment a thousand times. With every brushstroke, she pulled harder and harder. Each pull gave her a perverse satisfaction, a tinge of understanding of the horrible life she endured.

Facing the mirror reminded her that no one knew or understood her own pain. As she stared at the bun in her hair, she could only feel her sadness and despair.

These thoughts divided her against herself just like the strong part down the middle of her head. As Elise stared, it was a flash from the past ripping at her soul. She couldn't comfort herself or undo the pain. The pain was always there. A prison sentence, with no fixed end.

Why? Why? Why? It was extremely unfair. And the guilt was included on top of the confinement. How could it have been her own fault?

As her eyes glazed over through the tears, reality poked her, like a sword into her heart. Something crashed in the distance, the sound of breaking glass with a horrid scream. Yet she couldn't look away. The sad broken woman begged her to stay with her. It was as if the world had frozen. She couldn't afford any solace. The fear she faced of a crying desperate child should surely be enough to stop this trance. Reality wanted her attention.

But as she looked deeper, the sound was a memory. It was a moment she had forgotten. The moment her brother broke grandmother's vase. It was the moment of truth for him, but instead he was so quick with the blame. Grandmother never believed her. It wasn't fair. That awful day had been buried with all its terrible resentment.

Over and over again bad things seemed to push into her life. The woman in the mirror reminded her of this fate. There were no bright days. There was no walking on sunshine. There was only this fear of what was next? What next could go wrong?

Like the lines on the palm of her hand, the forehead wrinkles suddenly appeared. The deep worry and the deep disappointment permanently marked. As she waited and waited for all the good in life like a train speeding along the countryside, the wrinkles appeared.

She'd never paid attention to the worry lines or the anger lines on her forehead. But there they were staring at her with a sense of accomplishment. They were making a statement that this was her life. They were a roadmap of grief that was unimaginable or known to anyone. The pain she endured day after day was consuming. Now these reflected lines reminded her of the line across the sand that no one was allowed to cross.

Perhaps it was no surprise Elise ignored this woman behind the mirror. The lines were frightening. They could never be washed away, and only reflected her deep dark secrets.

Soon the glance in the mirror transformed into a trance. Unfortunately, it was more of an unwelcomed guest. In a shadow behind, an unexpected creature appeared. She was hallucinating now as this moment of quiet was a time-lapse within a time-lapse. The creature created a burning sensation in her skin. She recognized the shadow. It was the memory of an angel, a plastic doll who had come to life. Even though it was only a shadow, it was the memory of hope that she envisioned as a child. It was the angel of protection that disappeared years before.

This angel had made her smile. When she had questions as a youth, the angel was there for her. They were best friends. They were inseparable. They knew one another well. They read each other's minds. She never forgot. She often wondered why the angel disappeared. But now in the corner, the angel was a shadow quietly waiting to understand. This was more than she could comprehend. More tears rolled down her face. What was the truth? What was real? It had been so long. The memories were never erased, only set aside in hope of her dreams.

The shadow overstepped itself by appearing today. There was no closure. No goodbye, just a sad ending to all the hopes and happiness Elise desired. The shadow was a reminder that happiness was a figment of her imagination. The shadow bowed its head as the drape in the window moved from a cold breeze from outside. It disappeared and this connection disappeared. The shadow was a made-up creation, locked in her mind, a make-believe friendship.

As the shadow disappeared, she wondered if she was worthy of this attention. There was no hope other than enduring this dark prison sentence created for her own reality.

In that moment, the church bell rang and the trance was ended. Reality struck her as she prepared for bed. Today was Elise's birthday. It was her special day that went forgotten–just another day in Minnesota. Another cold blustery day added to this winter blizzard, where others had needed her. The bitterly cold winter day had finally ended. It was a day unnoticed and forgotten because she was here to serve her family and her congregation of this country church. Only the mirror knew the lifetime of pain she saw in the reflection.

Maybe surviving the day was not the chapter that was written for her. Maybe this was not the story she was supposed to live. As she looked in the mirror, she saw a stranger staring back at her. Was she was living someone else's life as she looked in the mirror?

 Lisa Carmichael is an entrepreneur and marketer who lives with her family in Minnesota. She writes from her laptop and transcribes from her journal. Lisa has a passion to help entrepreneurs develop strong relationships with their customers allowing their business to stand out from the competition.

Broken Class:
A Sci-Fi Fantasy Story

TERESA FOUSHEE

1 The End

To begin with, Dad was dead. He died just before the Big Change. I could have been there with him for his last breath, but Mom was there, and the wedge was too big for Mom and me to be in the same room at the same time. So, I was in my home studio, doing what I could to feel close to him, composing and recording comforting music with my synthesizer, making music that could be played softly in his room.

I remember suddenly feeling a presence, like eyes on me, intently gazing and waiting for me to notice them. I stopped playing and looked around, expecting to see someone there, but the room was empty except for me. It was Dad's presence I felt, and my heart broke a little bit, sad there would be no more new memories to make with him, but glad he was free from pain. Part of me felt guilty I was not in that room with his body, but I was glad he could see that he was on my mind and in my heart. Maybe that was why he came.

"Hi, Dad," I said softly to the empty room while the hair on the back of my neck stood up and my skin tingled.

"Hi, honey," he said gently, but not out loud. I heard his voice speaking to me inside my head. I didn't give it much thought at the time because I was so glad Dad came to me. So much had happened and it felt good to experience pure love in that moment.

I sighed. "I'm sorry I didn't get this music to you in time for you to enjoy it."

"I'm sorry I didn't take time before now to have this talk with you," he said.

"What? Dad—*Please*, not the birds and bees," I said, squinting my eyes shut while drawing back.

"No, not that talk. This is a different one ..."

"Oh. Sure. Dad. Don't worry. I love you, and I know you love me too. And I know we don't talk about feelings in our family. *So* Minnesota. *So* Midwest. *So* reserved, right? It's okay though. I love you. You can go... Into the light..." I smiled weakly.

"Well, thank you, honey, for loving me. I love you too." He paused and then continued slowly. "This is about something else. You know I enjoyed making super computers at United Systems, getting them up and running at client sites, and ..." his voice trailed off as if he left me to be with his memory, and then he returned to me. "You remember the end of the night at card parties when I recalled the cards everyone played that night?"

"Sure Dad. I know you liked your job." He loved his job. I drifted back in time to when every big corporation had entire floors dedicated to hold the super computers of the day. It was a time when specialists, like Dad, were sent to solve problems and get them up and running…when the world was not virtual. I returned to Dad. "And you were like a magician at card parties, but… no offense here… it seems a little weird to be talking about card games."

"Remember when I taught myself to speak all those languages: Japanese, Norwegian, German, Spanish?"

"Yeah," I said, moving mental jigsaw puzzle pieces around.

"Well, I never told you, or Mom, that United Systems outfitted me with a neural enhancing device a long time ago as part of a project I worked on. I agreed to it if they agreed to give you one too."

"WHAT?!" My brain got stuck.

"Don't worry, honey, it's not online yet. You won't connect until your 25th birthday."

I would turn 25 that week, but hadn't thought about it with everything going on with Dad. My brain stopped dead in its tracks. Locked up. Shut down. I could not think. *Could. Not. Think.*

Then I felt a shiver, and I was ready to jump up and run or punch something.

He barely paused before continuing, "Someone will find you in a few days and you need to go with them. They will teach you how to use it and keep you safe while you learn. Remember: You can always talk to me. You won't see me or hear me, but I will see you and I will hear you and respond somehow. I love you. And nothing can ever change that. I. Love. You."

And then. Nothing. I felt warm. And sad. Sad that my dad's life was done. And then I stopped feeling. And then.

I just. Stopped. I looked down at my keyboard and stared at nothing, letting out a long deep sigh that went forever.

My phone rang and the caller was identified as Mom. Right. I took a breath in, held it a few beats, and then squeezed all the air out of my lungs. Then I took a normal breath before answering, "Hi Mom."

"Tess, Dad quit breathing." She went on in a pitch too high to be authentic. "I'm sorry I didn't call you sooner, so you could be with him at the end."

I stiffened at the sound of her voice as she continued. "Would you like to come now and sit in the room? Maybe bring your keyboard and play something?"

"Sure, Mom. I'll come right now."

❖

In the days that followed I moved through the grief fog as my birthday came and went amid the service, condolences, and acknowledgements. The end-of-life markers.

❖

It happened a month after my 25th birthday, while I was out running on a trail. I walked out my front door, crossed the street, and ran the winding asphalt path for a half mile, traffic on my left and woods bordering the park reserve on my right. Then I took the secret right turn down the hill and into the woods, half-run-half-walk, focused on my footing to avoid falling down the rocky slope. The surroundings transformed from urban to hilly, wooded, wetland wildness, and at the bottom of the slope, the trail connected to a network of trails shared by more deer and rabbits than people. I felt connected to the earth and to myself with each step.

I was running up a hill, breathing hard, and kept myself going by chanting out loud to drown out the resistant voice in my head. "Keep going!" *This is hard.* I got to the top. "Good work!" *This is so hard.* "You're doing great! Keep going!" The sun greeted me as I ran into a clearing at the top of the hill before heading back down the hill. Suddenly I felt a presence.

"Hi, Tess. I'm Homer and I'll be working with you now."

I looked around and kept running. No one behind me, just trees left and right.

I bolted to outrun whoever or whatever spoke to me. I came to the rocky downhill stretch ahead of me and heard:

"Tess—Wait!" But it was too late.

I stumbled and tumbled and went down the wrong way. I tried to get up.

Homer's voice cut in low and slow, "Tess, stop."

"Listen to me. You fell. You're hurt. Be still. We're going to help you."

I tried again to get up, but couldn't move. Why couldn't I move? I tried to focus, but I couldn't see. Why couldn't I see? Who was Homer? *What the hell was going on?*

Then, as if speaking to someone else, Homer said, "Scan indicates she's got a fractured skull and pelvis. There is swelling, and bleeding, pulse is rapid, but faint, skin is clammy... Affirmative, need a trauma team on arrival... Scan picked up her signal and I pinged her bit, but I can't connect to root, not sure why... Right, see if you can get remote access, login to root and get her online while we wait for transport... You got a lock? ... Good. Two to transport on your ready."

———— ❧ ————

2 The Stirring

I wake up, but before I open my eyes, I try to move.

Okay. First. Toes. Move the toes.

I feel my toes wiggle.

Okay. Good. Now move the feet, the ankles, and the legs.

I feel my toes point down, then flex the feet and curl the toes up, both ankles circle in, then out, then stop. I feel my legs wiggle back and forth.

Okay! Good! Now, open the eyes and look at the hands.

I open my eyes and delight in the sight of my fingers, and I promise I won't ever take them for granted, knowing that I will take them for granted again. But not right now. Right now, my awareness is focused on gratitude.

"Online and—" Wait, what did I say? Did I say that?

"—Connected."

I know I did not say that! A voice in my head that was not mine... Wait a minute... I feel a presence.

My brow is furrowed. "Who said that?" I ask out loud.

"Said what?" says the voice in my head.

Wait a ... *Minute!*

"Homer. The voice mask worked, then it failed. We need to reboot."

Homer's late night deejay voice cuts in again, "Tess, we need you to be still again. Then you can get up and move around."

We? *Who is We?*

<hr/>

I woke up again and opened my eyes. Everything in the room was a shade of white: the walls, the ceiling. But no windows. Light everywhere, and everything emanated light. Not harsh light. Easy-to-take-in light. I was in a bed in a room. Where was I? My pulse quickened.

"You are in the care center. You are recovering. Good work."

I looked around and saw no one. It was unnerving and I was getting annoyed.

"Looks like it's hard for you not seeing faces to go with voices. You are online now, with your neubit helping you recover. Keep going," said the voice.

"Thank you. What's a noobit?"

"Homer will explain. You're doing great."

"Hi Tess." The voice sounded like a late-night radio deejay voice. "This is hard. You're getting better, and you're doing great. I understand you're getting tired of faceless voices. How do you feel?"

"Okay. It feels like others see me, but I can't see them. Awkward."

"Got it. Let's explore this. You fell and your injuries were serious. For now, think about things this way... Your system can accelerate recovery by resting non-essential sub-systems. Sight is not essential to this phase of your recovery, so it's resting."

Okay.

"Bones are the focus of your recovery—fractured skull, and hip. They've healed enough that you can get up and walk around. Maybe in a week or two you can run. You've been through a lot, but we need to keep going. What did your father say about your neubit?"

"He never called it a *new bit*, or *noobit*, or whatever you call it... What did you call it?

"Neubit. Like neuron and computer bit. Neubit."
"Oh, okay. Neubit. He didn't call it that. He just told me he had a neural enhancement device and that he got me one too, and that someone would find me and teach me how to use it. Is the neubit the neural enhancement device?"

"Yes, that's right. Good work. I'll teach you how to use it. Let's start right now." Homer continued, "You don't have to understand physics to turn on an engine and drive a vehicle or use a computer. You just fire it up and go. Same with your neubit. Technically, it's a neuro-bit. Sometimes we just call it a *bit*."

"Does everyone have a bit?"
"No, they do not."
"Why?"
"They are expensive."
Hm. I nod my head slowly, "Okay. What's next?"
"Let's play a game. Without trying too hard, lift your hands and look at them."
I lifted my hands so I could see them.
"Good. Now tell me what you see."
"I see fingers, thumbs, and the backs of my hands."
"Good. Zoom in. Now, tell me what you see."
"I see fingers. Fingernails. I see edge of nail, body of nail, side fold, cuticle, root, matrix."
"Good work. That's enough for today. Rest. We will resume tomorrow."

Over time Homer taught me to use the neuro-bit to sharpen my senses and build strength, starting with vision, and hearing. The deeper I went the more I could sense. Like layers of an onion. Like increasing magnification with a microscope or using a high-speed camera. Soon I could pick up vibrations from plant leaves and my brain translated it into music or whatever sound was stored in the vibration.

Then Homer announced it was time to move up a level. "You can sense. You are doing great. Now it's time to introduce you to the neuro-network."

"The what? Neural network?" I learned about neural networking a million years ago, back when artificial intelligence was new.

"Neuro-network, or neuron network, or neuro-net, or net." Homer paused then resumed. "Think of it like being in a dark room with one point of light shining on one object. Your job is to focus on seeing the object. Sounds easy, right? When you direct your attention to one object, it's easier to do when you focus on that one object, listen to your breath, and let go of thoughts. It's harder to do when you follow one thought after another. You can get lost in thought and lose sight of the only object in the room. Now think of a room filled with infinite sources of light shining on infinite objects of all kinds. The same principles apply, even though it seems more complex. So it is with your bit on the net. With many lights and objects, how do you determine where to focus and for how long? Now add the other human senses. Time for an exercise. Your filters will be turned off and you will experience full unfettered access to the net. Then filters will be turned back on. It will only be for a moment. You can do this. Set timer to one second. Start on your ready."

Suddenly I sensed everything in the room and everywhere all at once in what I can only describe now, as an assault. My senses transitioned from perceiving what was in my room to perceiving everything that is and in that one second. Like balancing an entire solar system on the head of a pin. A cacophony of what seemed like a whirling broken kaleidoscope swirling around the senses. It was loud and quiet, harsh and soft, stench of death and stink of birth, whispers and screams, flashes of harsh light alternating with flashes of dense darkness. Beings of every imaginable kind cycled through my awareness, overwhelming my senses, inducing a kind of paralysis, like the cartoon bomb, motionless, waiting for the spark to travel the path of the shrinking fuse, tension mounting until the spark kisses the bomb and ignites an explosion. Like a room filling with natural gas—you can't see danger, but you can sense it, and you have learned, hopefully not from experience, it's not a good place to light a match.

Just as suddenly I was back in the room. Quiet. Womblike. Safe. I fell into the bed, exhausted.

Over time Homer taught me how to focus, direct, and filter out the never-ending stream of electrical impulses that surrounded me, that surrounds all beings, and I learned to navigate the neuro-network. Kind of like navigating the state fair. An ocean of life. An experience of sights, sounds, tastes and smells that come together, where each being travels, for better or worse, in the direction of their dreams ... or nightmares.

3 The Beginning

Dad got me the neurobit and Homer got me connected to the neuronet. But Mom had introduced me to the most powerful network before I knew what it was: the social network. Sure, the neuronet is capable of powerful feats, but it's only as capable as the underlying network of beings working together. Social networks have always been and will always be. It was Mom's network, powered by the people she connected with, that moved mountains before I could see them.

It was *her* family network that showed me how to love music. *She* encouraged me to learn to play the clarinet. After I advanced to first chair in honor band and begged for a piano, s*he* searched for a piano in *her* church network. *She* heard about an old, free, beat-up upright piano. *She* found people to help get that old piano home. *She* discovered my piano teacher. *She* encouraged me to practice, letting me skip dishwashing after dinner to play piano. *She* made Dad drive her to attend my every band concert and recital. *She* offered to get me a guitar and lessons...

But by then it was too late. I disconnected from her. Despite my claims of a revolution, I saw what I was told to see and heard what I was told to hear by a network vested in its own self-preservation. I believed I would benefit in their service and served at my expense. I aligned what I perceived as truth and squished my own soul. I was rewarded for obedience, but my soul withered until it became compost.

I remember that hand-me-down upright piano in the living room. Beat up on the outside. It made a deep, rich and soulful sound, pure love vibrating out from strings that stirred my soul.

I keep going. I question what I know to be true and open myself to new evidence, which sometimes leads me to new answers and new questions. Small acts of pure love change the world. Regardless of who initially gets the credit.

All I have to do is connect.

Hi Mom. It's me, Tess. I love you. Thank you.

Teresa Foushee earned degrees in computer science and accounting and founded an information technology company serving Fortune 500 companies. After deaths in her world cracked her heart open, she left the corporate world to explore creative answers to old questions. Composing songs on piano originally for herself, she was invited to perform on stage, record, and license her music. Her literary work is published in magazines and anthologies, and she is now writing and illustrating her first book for kids, *Into the Air* about a fish who decides to fly; Fran aims high and never gives up. Learn more at www.PosiVibes.com

Story 4

The Carnival

Alana Faulk

❖

Her foot slipped back and forth rapidly from the accelerator to the brake pedal. Traffic out of Minneapolis was maddening on Friday afternoons, especially as the final days of the summer season drew near. Everyone struggled to squeeze in all of the things they had planned and intended to accomplish before Labor Day; and now here they were, with the unfinished list still looming, celebrating the final weekend of summer. This had been an eventful year for her. In fact, she had accomplished more this summer than she had in the past two decades combined.

To say she had come out of her shell would be a reasonable description, though maybe a bit modest. She had finally liberated herself from the self-imposed prison that had stifled her life for far too long. After losing well over 200 pounds she'd experienced a reincarnation of sorts, a reawakening, a rebirth. It had been a prolonged and lengthy process, which, she realized, was ongoing. It had taken her many years to feel strong enough to face the world once again. She had not crossed the finish line by any means, but she was back in the race, where even last place was exhilarating. She felt her mind, and her spirit growing stronger, ever expanding, as her body reduced and condensed itself. She thought she might have discovered the fountain of youth somewhere along the journey, for she felt younger and more invigorated as days slipped by. She began going places and doing things she had not even considered just a short time ago. She felt alive.

As the little car crept along 35W in rush hour traffic, she twisted the air conditioning knob once again, which still did absolutely nothing. The sun beat down on her through the windshield, making her feel like a bug under a magnifying glass. She needed out of this scorching hot car, at least until this 5 p.m. rush hour absurdity had subsided. She looked ahead and noticed the colorful flags rippling in the wind. A blue and yellow Ferris wheel rolled lazily in the sky. *A carnival,* she thought out loud, and without hesitation she yanked the steering wheel to the right and skidded across the gravel, down the exit ramp and into the busy parking lot, horns blaring and blasting behind her. She had not ventured through the gates of a carnival since she was a young girl, but the kid inside her whispered, "Today is the day."

As she sauntered past the "Mid-American Midway" ticket booth, a flirtatious concoction of delightful scents and smells engulfed her entire being. Hot buttered popcorn, mixed with warm, sticky cotton candy and foot long hotdogs simmering on the grill overwhelmed her senses, and it took great restraint and control to stroll past the enthusiastic vendors without stopping to sample any of the tempting treats. She had spent three years preparing for this battle and she moved along with confidence.

She had forgotten how overwhelming the magical world of the midway was. The numerous sights, sounds and smells overloaded one's senses. The peculiar music from the various rides and attractions traversed upon the muggy air in an eerie drone, sounding much like a warped record playing on a very old phonograph machine. She stood and watched the white horses of the carousel bob up and down while the children riding pompously upon them squealed in delight. As she worked her way towards the center of the tiny self-contained community, she came upon the games of chance. "All down...all ready...all ready...all down," the carnival barker yelled out to his customers who were frantically placing bets on their favorite colors as he reached up to spin the giant wheel of chance. In the booth next to him children tossed small wooden rings at long neck pop bottles...the sound of *tink...tink...tink* filled the air as the rings continuously bounced off the bottles, provoking the disappointed tykes to shell out yet another torn and tattered dollar bill in hopes of winning a stuffed teddy bear. As she stood and watched, temptation once again crept upon her. Elephant ears, deep fried Oreos and Funnel cakes the bright neon sign exclaimed! She did not need a sign to attract her attention. She recognized this sweet temptation long before the blinking billboard ever came into view. The intoxicating aroma made her head swim and she decided it might be best to turn and head in a different direction before this mounting craving got the best of her.

Behind her, she heard the distinct, unmistakable *click...click...click* of an ancient roller coaster straining to ascend the highest peak of the track. She glanced over her shoulder just in time to see the "Dizzy Dragon" climb up and over the hill, rushing rapidly down the other side as little hands flew up into the air and riders gasped and screamed in joyful terror. She smiled in a fleeting moment of recollection, remembering that the roller coaster had been her favorite ride as a child and even a young adult...until she had grown too large to lower the safety bar over her protruding belly. She turned and began moving once again. She strolled past the Funhouse and a wildly spinning ride called the Vertigo and, glancing up, found herself directly in front of the towering Ferris wheel. She stared up at the twenty or so bucket seats rocking empty in the wind and thought how exhilarating and free it must feel to tower above the Earth. She had not attempted to board any type of amusement ride such as this, since the afternoon she had been forced to climb out of the con- stricted roller coaster seat for being too "large" for the ride. She'd walked back down the up-ramp with her head down in shame as she struggled to hide her crimson cheeks from the cruel and laughing children.

She looked up once more, and with her heart racing, she strolled over to the little red-and-white striped ticket booth and handed the woman a $5 bill. "Just one." She stated, with a tiny quiver in her voice. She took the ticket and her change and headed back to the giant spinning wheel. The grubby looking carnie smiled at her and she could not help but notice the vacant spot in his grin where his front tooth had been. She smiled back as he took the ticket and led her up the shaking metal ramp. She took a deep breath as she stepped up into the bucket, politely ig- noring the greasy outstretched hand extended to help her.

She sat down on the hot vinyl seat and felt her heart stop beating as the carnie reached up to close the safety bar. She exhaled uncontrollably as the bar snapped easily into place. She sat up straight and rested her arm across the back of the gently swaying seat. As the magnificent machine jerked into motion her heart swelled in gratitude and appreciation for this second chance at life that she had so graciously been granted. She beamed an enormous smile as she reached what felt like the top of the world. She looked out through the shimmering heat waves and could see for miles around, the beautiful state of Minnesota. *The world is mine* she whispered under her breath, and she raised her hands above her, laughing uncontrollably as she headed back down.

Alana Marie is a Minnesota author, whose tales and yarns are based on actual events that have occurred throughout her very colorful life. Some of the stories may revolve around the trials and tribulations of friends and family but all include some shred of truth. Alana, herself, is an out and proud lesbian who once weighed 528 pounds. A former bar and nightclub owner with a serious infatuation for food and alcohol, she has overcome tremendous obstacles throughout the years. Now sober for more than a decade, she has published two books on Amazon under *the Pick a Struggle Cupcake* title. Alana has also been published in *Chicken Soup for the Soul* and *WW Thin-line magazine.* In sharing experiences and recovery in a raw, yet sensitive fashion, she hopes to inspire, provoke and motivate others to take the steps necessary to chase their dreams and conquer their own demons and dilemmas. Enjoy her stories and struggles...they come from the heart.

Cody, the Contrary Canine

KATHLEEN J. PETTIT

"Because every boy should have a dog," the client said. "I am giving your son, Tony, this beautiful whippet. He is six months old, house trained, and has impeccable lineage. I know you will all come to love him."

And that is how Cody became a member of our family. He was an elegant dog, almost dainty in appearance, white with a brindle saddle. His big brown eyes melted our hearts. And he didn't bark. He was an oddity in our central Minnesota town. Dogs in our hometown were large, hairy, manly beasts whose bark struck fear in strangers. Cody was a whippet, bred for speed, deviousness and thievery. He was not a dog who cuddled, and he didn't play. He wouldn't fetch balls, sticks, or Frisbees—the things ordinary dogs did. What he liked to do was to run as fast as he could or eat anything he could find. Best of all he liked to find a nice warm, soft spot to curl up for a snooze

Cody was a fair-weather dog. This was a problem in Minnesota. If it was too hot, too wet, or too cold, he refused to go outside. That happens to be the standard state of weather in Minnesota. The extent of this problem became evident one spring day when the temperature was 78 degrees, and a gentle rain was falling. I took him to the door to let him out to do his duty. He looked at me, then at the rain, then at me again. He would not budge. I tried cajoling him with kind, funny words. I tried bribing him with his favorite treat. I tried dragging him through the door. He was unmovable. And then he squatted. And peed. On my shoes. I ended up with tennis elbow trying to rub his nose in the pee that splashed on the floor. It took me months to heal my elbow, but it taught me a lesson. Don't believe the "experts" when they tell you dogs don't like their own pee or poo on their noses.

As I mentioned earlier, Cody liked to eat. This dog loved his pee and poo. Particularly his poo, and I was thoroughly grossed out by this habit. It was bad enough that he executed nighttime raids on the cat box but what was so disgusting is I rarely had to clean the yard of the dog doo because he ate it. This made his breath stink. I consulted the experts. They advised me to go out with him and pick it up immediately after he did his duty. That is fine advice, if you only had one dog to supervise, but I had three children, a husband, and three cats to tend to as well. They had needs. They had wants. And, oh, incidentally, I had needs and wants as well. But, I did my best to follow the dog around the back yard. He was very crafty. The minute my attention was averted, he did his thing and slyly walked away, saving it for later. Another solution the experts gave was to sprinkle his doo with cayenne powder. He liked that. I kept trying to find hotter sauces, thinking my 30-year-old spice probably had lost its efficacy. But the hotter the sauce, the more he liked it. I gave up. After all, I had a nice clean back yard. Cody cleaned it up for me.

Cody was a chewer. Those balls, sticks, and Frisbees we tried to get him to fetch didn't last long. He would find a sunny corner in the yard and turn them into confetti. When he got bored with the outdoor toys, shrubs, sticks and stones, he attacked Tony's stuffed animal collection in the house. Every single one had its nose chewed off. Next, he went after their eyes. Soon, there were no faces left on his collection. After Cody decimated Tony's stuffed animals, he moved on to the other children's stuffys, and then dolls, toys, shoes, clothes, soda pop, soup, tuna fish and vegetable cans, furniture legs, pillows, cushions, quilts ... whatever he could get into his mouth.

The children all hated the dog. I disliked the dog intensely, so I decided to consult the local vet as to what to do about him. He informed me the best thing to do was to put him down as he was an alpha dog and would not ever recognize a human being as his master. If I wasn't willing to do that, I was to continue putting hot sauce on the cat's and Cody's doo doo. That should eventually break that habit. The children will just have to take better care of their toys and I would just have to keep putting the dog out to do his potty. He will get used to it. So much for expert advice. Maybe it was the times. Maybe today, Cody would be seeing a psychologist. Maybe I would. I did not have the dog put down. What kind of message was that to my children? The dog is a little naughty so kill him? I was not about to give up.

Cody was an escape artist. He liked to hang out with me in the house, but if I needed to leave the house, I had to confine him to a space where he couldn't do any harm. That happened to be the kitchen. The kitchen had two doors to it: one regular door into the family room and two half doors that met vertically in the middle. This door exited to the foyer and the rest of the house. On this door, I put a hook lock. After several stays in the kitchen the dog figured out how to open the cupboard and refrigerator doors. I put baby locks on the lower cupboards and put chairs in front of the refrigerator. He figured out how to defeat the baby locks so I moved all food items in the lower cupboards up to the back of the counter tops. When that didn't work, I moved the food to the upper cabinets with baby locks. That worked. Next, he figured out how to move the chairs in front of the refrigerator at the same time that he figured out how to open the double doors with the hook lock. We believe that he stood on his hind legs with one front paw on one side door and the other paw on the second side door and gently pressured each door until the lock popped. Now he could raid the refrigerator and escape the kitchen. The contents of the refrigerator would be strewn all over the house, some found immediately, other food items days and weeks later because of the delightfully odiferous smell they projected.

Clearly, the kitchen would not do. So, I decided that when I left, I would leave the dog outside in the fenced-in back yard. He escaped by jumping the fence and wandering the neighborhood, which meant I was out looking for him and trying to capture him by enticing him with food. He figured that out very quickly, so I needed to find another solution. Chasing him didn't work as whippets are pound per pound one of the fastest animals on earth. He could run 35 miles per hour. The speed limit in my neighborhood was 25 miles per hour. My final decision was to just let him run until he came home. He always did. No one else could catch him either, not even the dog catcher.

Why didn't you put him in a cage, you might ask? Well, my husband didn't believe in cages. They were cruel, he thought. Never mind that dogs are den dwellers. But, after the Easter incident, he changed his mind. For Easter, my husband found the most exclusively delicious gourmet chocolate shop in the city. He bought all the Easter candy there: eggs, bunnies, everything you can imagine. He spent a fortune. Easter Eve, he put them in baskets and set them on the fireplace mantle. With the hearth in the way, he was sure Cody couldn't get the baskets. When we went to bed, he brought Cody upstairs and put him on his dog bed and then shut our bedroom door almost all the way. He inadvertently left just a crack open, sure that we were all secure in the bedroom. But not Cody. A crack was all he needed. As soon as we were all asleep, he went downstairs to the family room and figured out how to get that chocolate off the mantle. Not only did he get it down, he ate every last drop of it. He should have died. He should have gotten terribly sick. All he got was a little diarrhea, which was just fine with him because remember his obnoxious habit? He got to eat the chocolate twice or even thrice. We bought a cage.

Whippets were bred to be thieves. Not only are they as fast as the wind, they also have extraordinary eyesight. They can see moving animals from a very long distance. Our family had to keep track of Cody whenever we opened a door to the outside world. If Cody spotted something moving, he was gone. This was particularly problematic if we were at our lake cabin. The normal refrain was "where is Cody" before anyone opened the door. We needed to be sure he was restrained. If not, the dog was gone. Like a cat, he brought us many treasures such as rabbits, squirrels, chipmunks, birds, and bats. My greatest fear was one day he would bring us a skunk. Thank heavens that did not happen. Sometimes he brought us steaks, packages of brats, fish heads, loaves of bread, and pizza packaging. He opened the doors of other cabins and helped himself to food from their counters and refrigerators. He tipped over garbage cans. He raided fish houses. He snatched food off grills. He outran shot guns and pitchforks. And he always came home looking as pleased as could be because he had done his job supplying the family with partially eaten food for the table.

When Cody was about one year old, we moved from small-town Minnesota to the metro area. I brought the dog and a couple of kids in one car with my husband, the cats, and the rest of the children in the other. We had bought a house about a mile from my sister's house. She had a dog run attached to the garage. The fencing was about nine feet tall. The top was open, but two canoes were stored on top of it. We decided this was a perfect place to keep Cody while we unloaded the truck with our furniture at our new house. As we were taking a break from heavy lifting, Tony yelled out "Cody's here!" Noooo. How could that be? He has never been here. How could he find us? But sure enough, there was Cody, trotting down the street, pleased as punch to have found us. We tied him to a tree but to this day, no one knows how that dog got out of the cage at my sister's house.

I attributed most of Cody's behavior to his being less than one year of age. I was confident that as he matured, things would get better. They did not. For 10 years we lived with this dog. In the end, he developed arthritis and a serious skin disorder that gave him a distinctive odor. The odor was probably a result of his goat-like eating habits. He developed anxiety so if he were left in a room by himself, he would pee or poo. The vet told me to put him on a lead in the breakfast room, a room with vinyl flooring, attach him to the round table base, give him a comfortable bed to lie on, lots of water and food, and he would be okay. There were sliding glass doors off this room that led to the deck and that let in a lot of sunlight. Cody moved his bed around the table to get the perfect amount of sunlight that would keep him comfortable. He got to do the thing he loved the best, snooze all day on a soft bed in the warm sunshine. He left us for doggy heaven, but he lives on in family lore. Everyone has a favorite Cody story. And, we are thankful that we did not take that first vet's advice. We all came to love him, misbehaviors, odors and all.

 Kathleen J. Pettit is an arts administrator, poet, and creative nonfiction writer. Currently, she is the vice-president of the National League of American Pen Women Minnesota Branch, and a member of the League of Minnesota Poets, Women of Words, Pink, and Federated Women's Club of Bloomington. She spends her time between Osakis, Shell City, and Bloomington, MN.

Danger at the Border
CHRISTINE KELLY

Lilly Eckhart heard the scream just as she finished filling the water sack that she, Emma and Olivia were going to bring back to the campsite.

"What was that?" asked Emma.

"I'm pretty sure that was my mom," Lilly grimly noted. "There's only one reason my mom would scream."

"Those men Border Patrol Agent Maguire warned us about yesterday must have shown up at our campsite," Olivia answered. They all stared back toward the woods, paralyzed with worry.

"Yeah."

"What now?" Emma asked.

"Now we see what we can do to rescue them. But first things first, we need to send up a red flare for help."

"Where are we going to get a flare?" Emma questioned.

"Not an actual flare, Emma. We need to send out a cry for help."

"What do you suggest?"

"What if we fill one of the canoes with kindling and leaves —?"

"— and start it on fire," finished Olivia.

"Exactly."

As they collected material for the fire, Lilly thought about the rest of her Girl Scout Troop back at the campsite. The troop had been together since kindergarten. Her mom, Sara Eckhart, had been one of the troop leaders. Rebecca Townsend, Olivia's mom, had been the other. Both she and Olivia had grown up camping with their families. Sara and Rebecca had passed along their love of camping to the rest of the girls in the troop. It had been Lilly's idea to top off their senior year in high school and their final year in Troop #1987, with this trip to the Boundary Waters Canoe Area. The troop had spent months planning this trip.

"Do you think this is enough?"

Looking at what they had collected, Lilly said, "Yeah. I think this should send up a pretty good smoke signal. Hopefully, someone notices it and calls for help. Let me grab one of the canoes."

Lilly slid the canoe back into the water and then walked it out to the point. She had been camping here in the BWCA since she was nine months old. Her dad had persuaded her mom that she wasn't too young, and by the time Lilly was eight, she and her father were plotting out their annual trips together. Lilly had persuaded the rest of the troop to take this route. It was one of her favorites. Knowing the area, she knew the island point would be the best place to release the canoe so it would have the best possible chance of being noticed by someone in the area.

Hopefully, the dark smoke would alert authorities and they would come to investigate.

Emma and Olivia began constructing the campfire using the sticks, leaves, and pine needles they had found. Lilly reached into her pocket for the lighter she always carried. It wasn't there.

"Well, crap."

"What's the matter?"

"I left my trusty lighter back at the fire ring."

Emma smiled, "Don't worry, I've got my emergency fire-starting kit." She reached into her pocket and pulled out the prescription bottle that the troop had repurposed as a container to carry matches. Creating the fire starter kits had been one of the projects they had done as first graders.

"I can't believe you still have that!" Lilly laughed.

"Your mom told us we'd never know when we'd need it. I've always kept it in my pocket whenever we went camping."

Once the fire was burning and producing a thick cloud of black smoke, Lilly pushed it out into the middle of the water. As the canoe silently slid away from the shore, all three girls sent up a prayer that someone would come.

"Come on. We need to find out what's going on back at camp."

Lilly crept up to the edge of the campsite where she spotted two men holding the troop at gun point. Her breath caught in her lungs at seeing a handgun pointed at her mom's face. Her dad had died five years ago, and just the thought of something happening to her mom, made tears pool in her eyes.

Not now, Lilly girl, you've got a rescue mission to put together, she thought. She remembered the self-defense class the troop had taken last year. During it, the instructor had taught them anything could be used as a weapon. Lilly found herself looking around at the campsite with an eye for what the others could use to help defend themselves. She noticed the cast iron skillet and Dutch oven which were sitting near the fire ring: definitely options. Ultimately, it would be up to her mom and the others to grab what they could. Lilly hoped that her friends remembered the lesson, too.

Lilly joined Emma and Olivia back in the trees.

"We need to give the others a diversion; something that will distract the gunmen, and maybe even split them up. We need to give the others an opportunity to take control of the situation," Lilly said.

"What about a bear?"

Lilly turned to Olivia, "A bear? Where are we going to get a bear?"

"I can actually make a pretty good bear noise, remember? If I can scare your mom, who is never fooled by anything, I should be able to distract those two thugs."

<hr>

As soon as Emma and Olivia were in place and ready, Lilly blew her duck whistle. While they were planning this trip, the troop had come up with the idea of using a duck call to alert each other to possible wildlife or danger. Olivia had suggested using the duck call so they didn't scare any of the wildlife. Their plan had worked beautifully yesterday morning when they had come upon a moose. Lilly was able to notify the others with only a blow through her duck whistle. Everyone had silently rounded the bend in the river to see a bull moose standing in the water, eating his breakfast. *Let's just hope this works as well today as it did yesterday*, she thought. She blew the whistle.

Olivia began hitting a stick against the ground making a noise like a bear rooting around. Then she began to growl, snort and huff. If Lilly didn't know it was Olivia, she could almost believe there really was a bear. Lilly kept her eye on the campsite, watching the two men's reaction.

"Go see what that is," said the man closest to her mom.

— ❧ —

Border Patrol Agent Scott Maguire had entered the BWCA through Entry Point 24 yesterday. He was one of a handful of agents who had been tasked with notifying campers in the area that the FBI suspected the Theischert brothers were attempting to flee the country through the vast and open area of the BWCA. The brothers were suspected of blowing up the federal courthouse in St. Paul last month. Maguire was making his way back to Entry Point 24, when he spotted the thick black smoke. He quickly called in the threat to the US Forest Service. After alerting the Forest Service, he immediately began steering his boat in the direction of the black cloud hoping to find that the cause of the smoke was not an out-of-control forest fire. As he drove, he considered all of the possible scenarios. The most obvious was a mismanaged campfire, however, none of the campers he had met yesterday had been inexperienced. In fact, he was surprised how many of them were well-seasoned BWCA enthusiasts.

Thinking about his encounters yesterday, he couldn't help but smile thinking of the Girl Scout Troop who had fed him dinner. Not only was their lasagna delicious, but they had also been high spirited, smart and funny. He was currently drawing near to the location of their campsite. He rounded the next bend and immediately spotted the canoe ablaze. He approached it quickly and found the canoe empty. He started searching the water, looking for anyone who had jumped ship. The water was calm. In fact, the entire surrounding area was peaceful. The fire was the only sound he heard. He maneuvered closer to the canoe. As he examined the fire, he observed the teepee structure. This fire had been deliberately set. He looked around again and couldn't see anyone. He got a sinking feeling in his gut. If he had to guess, the troop had started this fire and set the canoe adrift as an SOS signal. He immediately radioed the command post for backup. *Hang in there, ladies, I'm on my way.*

⁂

Lilly and Emma watched as the one gunman moved into the trees to investigate. They waited until he was deep enough into the tree cover that his brother couldn't see what was happening. As he neared their position, the two girls attacked him with thick tree branches they had found. Lilly aimed for his head, and Emma aimed for the back of his knees. They had decided getting him on the ground would be the best possible way to subdue him. Just as they had hoped, Emma's blow had dropped the man to his knees. Lilly hit him as his knees hit the ground. It was Olivia who managed to get one last whack at the man that rendered him unconscious. *One down, one to go,* Lilly thought.

--------⁂--------

Sara heard the duck call and knew Lilly and the other two girls were going to attempt a rescue. Sara wanted to yell at them to run and hide. It was bad enough the gunmen had five of them hostage, she didn't want the other three to be anywhere near the danger. She also knew there was no way she could stop them. If she called out, then the Theischert brothers would be alerted to their presence. She took a deep breath. If she couldn't stop them, then she needed to be prepared for whatever happened. She spotted the large cast iron Dutch oven pot. If she got a chance, she could grab it and use it to disarm one of the men.

Then Sara heard the "bear," and knew it wasn't a real bear. Over the many years she, Josh and Lilly had been coming here, she had rarely seen a bear. They tended to avoid people and were never loud. Then she remembered Olivia making the bear noises on one of their previous camping trips. She realized the three girls were providing them with an opportunity to take out the gunman.

Sara waited for the brother who was still pointing his gun at her and Rebecca to move his focus to the trees behind him. She held her breath as she sensed her scouts become more alert, preparing for the opportunity to end this ordeal.

The second brother had left the campsite and walked into the trees in the direction of the noise. They could hear him clomping through the trees and undergrowth, not making any effort to be quiet. Sara noticed the first brother quickly glance over his shoulder, but then refocus his gun on her. The group heard more noise coming from the woods. These sounds seemed different than the noise the second brother was making. Then they all heard one final sound.

"Ooompf."

Sara didn't know who made the noise, but she hoped it wasn't the girls. The brother near her turned his body toward the noise. This was her chance. She reached down and grabbed the handle of the Dutch oven and swung the heavy pot up and in the direction of the gunman. She managed to connect with his shoulder and knocked him slightly off balance. He staggered a few steps but managed to stay on his feet. Just as he was regaining his balance, Lilly flew out of the trees armed with a branch. As she drew near to the man, she swung her branch, aiming for his head. He managed to duck at the last minute and avoided being brained. When she didn't make contact with anything, Lilly stumbled from the force of her swing and fell to the ground at the gunman's feet.

"Stop!" he screamed. "No one move. The next person to move is dead."

All of the women froze and stared at the man holding the gun. Sara knew each one of them wanted to rush the man but were too afraid he would shoot them. She didn't want any of them to risk it.

The gunman reached down, grabbed a handful of Lilly's hair and pulled her to her feet. Lilly immediately reached up trying to loosen his grasp. He was taller and pulling her backwards, which kept her off balance. He was moving toward the trees.

"Where's my brother? What'd 'cha do to him?" he shouted.

No one answered.

"Answer me! Where is he?"

The silence was his only answer.

Sara looked into the trees to see if she could spot Olivia, Emma or the other brother. She saw movement at the edge of the trees and was surprised to find herself looking at Agent Scott Maguire.

<hr>

Agent Maguire saw Ted Theischert had one hand grasping Lilly's hair and his other holding a gun aimed at her head. Everyone else in the camp was frozen in position. Scott silently moved closer to Theischert's position. His plan was to bum rush the man and hopefully surprise him before he could harm anyone. He took one last look at the group around the campfire ring making sure they were all relatively out of the way. As he searched the group, he saw Sara Eckhart looking directly at him. He saw her barely nod her head and then turn her attention back to the man holding Lilly.

He heard Sara say, "Lilly, remember what your dad told you before we left. Just stay calm and relax."

He knew Lilly's father was dead. Sara was sending a message to her daughter and him. His opportunity to take the man down was here.

He watched as Lilly went completely boneless in the man's grasp and collapsed to the ground. Her captor was so surprised by her actions that he was caught off balance as he continued to hold her hair. Her weight propelled him forward. Maguire rushed out and tackled him to the ground. Scott tried to pin him down, but Theischert rolled them over. Scott rolled them again and as soon as he was on top, he clocked Theischert in the jaw. It didn't take long for the other man to fight back. Theischert drew back his arm and tried to connect with Maguire's jaw but he didn't have the right angle. The blow merely grazed Scott's jaw. They both moved to attack again when they heard the gun fire. The dirt not more than a foot away from them rose like a puff of smoke.

"I'm a pretty good shot at this range. I'd suggest you stop moving."

The gun shot was enough to stun Theischert. Scott hit him again. His second blow dazed the man just enough that Scott was able to flip Theischert over and grab his handcuffs. He wrapped the cuffs around the gunman's wrists. As soon as he had him contained, Maguire looked up and saw Sara holding the handgun. He smiled.

"Thanks for letting me do *something* here. If word got out that you completely subdued these two without any assistance from me, I'd never hear the end of it."

Sara didn't say a word. She just looked at him and smiled.

----------————☘————----------

It didn't take long for the campsite to be flooded with federal officers who quickly took the brothers into custody. Sara was so relieved that the whole ordeal was over and none of the girls had been hurt.

"How're you doin'?" Scott Maguire quietly asked.

"I'm not sure I'll ever get over the visual of that man holding a gun to Lilly's head."

"Yeah, I can imagine that was terrifying." He paused for a moment and then asked, "Are you going to stay?"

She turned and looked at him. He saw sadness and also the fear that still coursed through her system. She shrugged.

"I don't know how I can stay here for six more nights thinking about what almost happened."

"Mom, we can't go home! This was our last trip! It's our last time to be together before we all head off to college. Please let us stay," Lilly implored.

She moved toward her daughter and reached out her arms. Lilly fell into them. The two held onto each other, each looking for and giving comfort.

"Lilly, you could have —"

"I know, Mom. So could you."

Sara hugged her daughter closer hoping to blot out the horrible memory.

Scott cleared his throat.

"I have an idea."

Mother and daughter, still embracing, turned toward him.

"What if you had a bodyguard for the rest of the week?"

"A bodyguard?"

"I'd be happy to act as an escort for the remainder of the trip."

"Can you do that?"

"I actually had taken this week off but got called in when the Theischert brothers decided to make a break for the border. I wouldn't mind staying with you and looking out for you."

"Are you serious?"

"Would it help?"

Sara looked into the man's eyes and realized his presence would provide a sense of security she wouldn't have otherwise. She nodded.

He turned to the rest of the group. "What do you think? Mind if I tag along?"

"That would be a relief," Rebecca agreed.

"Are we really going to let a *guy* come along on this trip?" laughed Olivia.

"He can come, as long as he has to help with the caper chart," one of the other girls responded.

He smiled. "I don't mind helping with the chores, if I get another meal like last night's."

"I don't know, Mom, you always said not to feed the wildlife," Lilly winked.

"Although, I'm not a bear, I'm actually a pretty good fisherman. Can I stay if I provide dinner for a night?"

"Done," Lilly laughed. "Fresh fish is my favorite meal, but no matter how hard I try, I'm never able to catch anything worth keeping."

Stay tuned for the continuing adventures of Troop #1987, Sara Eckhart and Agent Maguire.

Thrown by Love's award-winning romance author C. Kelly reveled in the challenge of writing this short story and looks forward to expanding Scott and Sara's tale into a full-length novel. When she's not writing, she loves laughing and spending time with her family in Minnesota.

The Final Game

JUDITH F. BRENNER

M ary gripped her signed softball with two hands, her bony knuckles rotating it as she would a MAGIC 8 BALL®, ready to tell her which pitch to throw. Should it be a drop ball? Maybe a curve. Or she could surprise opponents with her famous drop screw ball! She hadn't been to a field in so long, but now, watching the game through the fence at a Minneapolis park from the vantage point of the catcher, she held the ball loosely, embracing the cloth as it rubbed her palms, the stitching tickling her thin skin.

An hour before, a fellow patient, Lenny, had set off the alarm bell when he opened the door for Mary. He pushed her wheelchair just enough to get her going, so she could wheel herself to the park one block away with the ball tucked between her legs. It was a signed ball that had been displayed in her hometown high school's trophy case. She told Lenny all about it that morning when he placed it in her hands from her shelf. He could read her mind. He was losing his.

A young volunteer student nurse, Jessica, entered the door to the memory care center, thanking Lenny for holding the front door for her. Being a Friday, his care team helped him dress in his red shirt buttoned to the top, resembling an usher at a theater. Jess met Lenny's unshaven face with a smile as he leaned on his cane, while she flashed her volunteer badge at the front desk clerk. Then Jess headed to see the first patient on her list: Mary, Room 106.

While the front desk clerk, Sarah, was sexting her boyfriend, Lenny was nodding his chin as if urging a butterfly away from a net, while Mary rolled down the walkway. His wrist band set off the motion detector. Sarah was oblivious that Mary had wheeled herself out of the building.

"Lenny, you know you can't go outside that way. If you want some fresh air, walk outside through the courtyard," she said, swiveling her chair to come around to the visitor's side. She gently led Lenny by the arm away from the door, letting it swing shut and lock.

Jessica walked back toward Sarah, concerned. "Excuse me, I'm looking for Mary Thompson. She's not in her room."

"Try the Courtyard. Follow that patient. That's Lenny. He's heading there now," Sarah said.

"Minnesocare Agency didn't provide a photo in the file. What does Mary look like?" asked Jessica.

"I couldn't tell you. Check the East wing desk. They know the patients better. I only recognize Lenny 'cause he tries to get out, so I keep watch."

At the field, a fast pitch whizzed over home plate, and the batter struck out. Mary clapped along with the other fans. The players reminded her of herself, and at the same time, her grandchildren. She twisted the ball in her hands, relishing the feeling. Mary raised her arm as high as she could, which arthritis stopped at chest level, but high enough to block the sun from her eyes so she could see the next pitch. Her heart pounded. She usually had such a weak pulse, but not today. Her family took advice from her doctor to put her in hospice care since her condition limited her from all activity except reading. At 95, she had plenty of memories of a healthy heart which raced in a healthy pattern when she pitched multiple no hitters and helped her high school team win the State Championship. She secured a scholarship to attend the University of Oklahoma, where again, she led the U's softball team in the Big 12 Conference. Now she felt 22 again, the sun hitting her face, the crowd yelling and jumping as a runner slid into home plate, the pitcher throwing in time for the out. No score. "We don't play with Barbie dolls. We play with bats and balls!" Mary sang and raised the softball with both hands, squealing in delight.

The effort was too much for her old heart. Her grip loosened. It fell to her lap, then tumbled to the pedals of the wheelchair. Her wrist band reflected beams of sun; a closed-mouth smile hidden as her chin slumped to her chest.

Judith F. Brenner is the author of *The Moments Between Dreams*, a novel (2022), and owns Creative Lakes Media, LLC, an editing services company. She is the managing editor and publisher of Sharpeners Report, a national publication. Her personal essays have been published in *Writers in the Know* literary magazine, and *Minnesota Parent*. She completed the Iowa University Mini-MFA Workshop (2019). Judith is a member of the Loft Literary Center, the Professional Editor's Network and the Chicago Writers Association. When she's not editing, reading or writing, you'll find her hiking in California (snow-bird) or gardening in Minnesota (summer-bird).

The Big Catch
COLLEEN BALDRICA

Summer was family vacation time. The year I turned seven I was going to learn how to fish. Mom and Dad packed the carrier on top of the station wagon with food, clothes, life jackets, tackle and fishing rods. Dad woke my brothers and me at 5:00 in the morning. The three of us carried our blankets and pillows, piled in the car and hunkered down for the five-hour drive. We were going to Battle Point Lodge on Leach Lake near Federal Dam.

My brothers and I slept a couple of hours. When we woke up, we were hungry. Dad was driving and said we'd stop for breakfast when we reached McGregor. We never went out for breakfast, so this was a treat. The cafe had stuffed fish on the walls and smelled like coffee and syrup. Mom said we could order anything off the kiddie menu. No cornflakes this morning, I was having pancakes. They had blueberries in them, and I put on lots of syrup.

A few hours later we were about twenty miles from the resort. The road was gravel and the bumps made it feel like a wild ride at the country fair. I wished I hadn't eaten the pancakes. My stomach was turning. I yelled, "Stop the car!" Dad slammed on the brakes, jumped out, opened the back door as those pancakes decided to leave my stomach. I threw up until nothing was left. Crying I asked, "Are we almost there?"

Driving over that last hill, seeing the lake and the resort, I forgot I felt sick. It was beautiful. The lodge and the cabins were made of logs. The dock stretched out for what seemed like forever. Fishing boats were lined up on each side. There were old tires on poles to keep the boats from hitting the dock. The air smelled like fish.

"We're here!" I yelled. Mom and Dad parked the car and went into the lodge to find our cabin number. They drove, while my brothers and I raced to cabin two. No way I was getting into that car again until we were heading home.

The cabin had a small kitchen, two bedrooms, one with three beds, and a living room with an old couch. I looked around. Something was missing. There wasn't a bathroom. I looked at Mom. She told me it was rustic and walked my brothers and me to the shower house. It wasn't far. There were two sides, one for the men and one for the women. Each had two toilet areas and one shower. "But Mom, I pee at night. Do I have to come out here?" I asked. She walked us back in the cabin and showed us this white covered pot that with a silver handle. She explained we'd pee in the pot at night and my job would be to carry it to the shower house to empty in the morning. Every night I tried to hold it in. Every morning I headed to the shower house with the bucket in hand.

My first day of fishing was exciting. I had little patience for everything that had to be done before I could even step into the boat. Impatiently, I watched as the dock boy took Dad to the bait house where he picked out minnows, worms, and leaches. Then they filled the gas tank, loaded the boat with poles, the tackle box and an extra bag. Finally, we were ready.

Standing on the dock with my life jacket on, Dad helped me into the boat. I sat in the front so I could watch where we were going. Dad started the engine while the dock boy released the boat. Off we went.

The boat hit the waves and bounced. We were heading to the clam beds. I didn't know anything about clam beds except that was where the walleyes were biting. Once there, I had to decide what bait I would use. The leaches were squirmy. And one curled around and latched onto my finger. I decided on a minnow. Dad said, "If you want to fish, you have to bait your own hook." He showed me once, then it was my turn. I put my hand in the bucket, grabbed a minnow, and held it tight with its mouth opened. The hook went in the mouth, out the gill, and into the upper back. Hook baited, I put my pole over the edge of the boat and lowered the minnow. I was ready.

Nothing happened. It was my understanding once the bait was in the water the fish would bite. Not so. I had to learn patience. Thank goodness the extra bag held candy bars and that I had Dad all to myself.

As Dad and I chewed our candy bars, my pole started to bend. "Let it be for a moment...Okay...Now pull back hard," Dad said. My pole was really bending, and I held on. "Give it some line. Thatta girl. Now hold your pole up and try to reel the line in." I turned the handle over and over. Dad got the net ready. Once the fish got to the side of the boat, he swooped down, securing the fish in the net. My first fish was a walleye! From that moment I knew, I loved fishing.

Every summer while growing up, I spent all my free time on the water: swimming, water skiing and fishing. I grew up on the St. Croix River and learned to swim right after I learned to walk. Maybe my love for water was because I'm part fish. Anyway, that was the joke I heard every time I went out fishing. Sometimes I'd keep the fish for dinner, mostly I'd catch and release. That's when you get the thrill of the catch without having the mess of cleaning them afterward.

After graduating college, I joined a fishing club. We fished lakes and rivers within a hundred miles of the Twin Cities. I had done most of my fishing on the St. Croix River, and Leach Lake during the summers. Now I wanted to experience other areas and meet more anglers. These outings focused on bass fishing: the equipment, the techniques, and the depth for best results. I learned a lot with that club, however, I wanted to catch walleyes and be a part of a team that would win tournaments.

Most tournaments required you to have your own boat. I didn't. I decided to be a co-angler, which meant I'd have to find someone willing to let me learn from them and eventually be their tournament partner. Lucky for me, my older brother had a friend with his own boat who was willing to teach me what he knew. If all worked out, I'd be his tournament partner.

Kegan, was about 6'4, 250 pounds. He had blond hair, was friendly, knew how to catch walleyes, and said fuck a lot. Kegan told me I needed to have my own equipment and made suggestions. I purchased a six foot, medium-light, fast-action spinning rod, with a size 30 spinning reel.

I put on eight-pound line, bought a number of jigs, and also candy bars for good luck.

Kegan's boat was a 17.5-foot Tuffy with a deep V design. It was spacious enough for us and equipment, had two live wells, a depth finder, and was powered by a 150 Mercury motor.

Kegan and I now had to see how we worked together before entering tournaments. We needed to become a team. Our first fishing outing was going to be a day on Mille Lacs. Kegan offered to have me drive up with him., but I declined. I figured we'd be in the boat all day, and I might want some alone time on the drive home. We met at the Spot Light Cafe in Garrison at seven for a quick breakfast.

During breakfast Kegan gave me my first lesson on finding walleyes. "Walleye aren't like other fish," Kegan explained. "Walleye navigate and hold according to the structure. Look for a point on the shoreline where shallow water protrudes out into the lake and then gets deeper. As it gets deeper, it often supports a rock pile. Walleye love points because they usually have multiple depths around a small area. Walleye seek deeper water during the day and feed shallow at night. A point starts shallow then transitions to a steeper drop. This reduces the distance walleye need to complete their daily routine. Walleye can feed in the rocky, sandy, or grassy areas during the dusk and dawn, then swim a few yards away to feed along the deeper area during mid-day."

Breakfast finished, I followed Kegan to the boat launch. We loaded equipment, put life jackets on, and headed out. The morning was overcast and cool, and the lake was choppy. Kegan knew this lake well, yet he looked at me and asked, "Where should we go?" He was testing me. I searched the lake and saw the land come to a point on the north side of the lake. I pointed. He smiled. We were on our way.

I sat in the front of the boat. It was an exhilarating feeling with the wind on my face as the boat jumped waves. I was in my happy place on the water and experiencing my first fishing trip with my future tournament partner.

We reached the spot. The depth finder showed the contour of the lake bottom and a bunch of large rocks. Because the waves were about a foot high, we decided to let the boat drift. This was the perfect place to drop a line.

I was using a bright florescent green jig along with a flathead minnow. I was jigging my line, which is a way of getting your bait near the bottom. Jigging is lifting your pole about a foot, dropping it back down, pausing on the bottom, repeat. You do this every three to five seconds because this is supposed to get the walleye to bite. Not sure who got in the walleye's head to know this. I was trusting Kegan's instructions. If I wanted to be his co-angler, I needed to prove I was listening.

"Walleye fishing takes patience. Learning how to fish for walleye can be frustrating," Kegan explained. Sitting in the boat we had lots of time to get to know one another. He was funny, about six years older than me, and had never been married. He explained that was because he hasn't met the right woman. "She has to love the outdoors, fishing, hunting and be willing to eat venison. I've met many nice women, but some don't eat meat. I believe you honor the animal by using as much of it as you can. Heck, it gave its life to feed you. Who wouldn't eat meat?" he asked me with a grin on his face. Laughing, I offered him a Snickers bar.

"You see that?" Kegan asked, watching my rod. "If you're hitting the bottom, you feel a gradual pull. When a walleye bites, it feels like a *tap-tap-tap*. See the rod tapping? It's a walleye. Get ready. When I yell "Now!" pull your rod hard up and to the left."

"NOW!" Kegan shouted. When I pulled up, my rod bent because the walleye was on my line. I held my rod up and reeled the line in slowly. As the fish neared the boat, Kegan had the net ready. I had just caught the first walleye of the day. It measured 14 inches. We were doing catch and release, so back into the water it went.

"Damn!" I yelled moments later, as the line snapped and my pole went limp. "Felt like a big one." "Too bad", said Kegan. "You had it. I think you gave him too much slack."

Fuck you, I thought, but looking at him, I smiled and said, "Yeah you're probably right." Being one of the few female anglers I needed to learn as much as I could, and Kegan was an excellent teacher. We fished a few more hours and caught three more walleyes.

Over the next month we went fishing at least twice a week. Sometimes we drifted, sometimes we used a trolling motor. I usually didn't use a bobber because it was more fun trying to feel the taps. One thing I needed to get used to was peeing off the side of the boat. Guys have it easy. I learned to pull my pants down just far enough to slide my butt off the side of the boat, pee and pull them up fast. Kegan always turned away, which made it less awkward. When you are fishing, no one takes a bathroom break at shore. You're out there for the long haul.

Kegan and I enjoyed each other's company and were content to sit in the boat, fish, talk, laugh, and eat candy bars. Surprisingly, I found myself thinking of him often when we weren't together.

Six weeks after our first outing, Kegan called to tell me he signed us up for a walleye tournament in Detroit Lakes. The tournament was one day, 7:00 a.m. to 4:00 p.m. 50 teams, with an entry fee of $400 per team. I was so excited I screamed. He reminded me I needed to pay half of the entry fee, lodging, gas and bait bill. "No problem!" I shouted.

The tournament was two weeks away and there was still so much for me to learn. What exactly was the co-angler's role? I knew it was a great learning experience and Kegan had been wonderful. "Am I supposed to do more?" I asked Kegan. He said, "No. We'll be a team and split any winnings." I knew this was more than most co-anglers get. We'd be using his boat, his equipment. I was just bringing my rod, reel, tackle box and candy bars. A sweet deal and I was all for it.

A few days before we were to travel the four hours to Detroit Lakes, we met at the boat to make sure we were ready. Together we checked everything: the live tank, motor, and the depth finder. We went through our tackle boxes and found I needed some extra line, a few more weights and jigs. I drove to Cabela's to pick up what I needed.

Kegan and I drove to Detroit Lakes the night before the tournament. We put the boat in the water and searched the lake for landmarks. We shared a room, Kegan in his bed and me in mine. The alarm was set for 4:30 a.m.

I was so excited but still managed five hours of hard sleep.

When the alarm went off, I ran to the bathroom first, took a fast shower, dressed and was ready to go. I told Kegan I'd meet him at the restaurant across the street. When he arrived, I had already ordered coffee and the breakfast special for both of us. We needed a hearty breakfast, and I was paying.

Kegan explained how the day would go. "The bell will ring, and all the boats take off. The fish need to be at least 14 inches in length and kept in the live well. At the end, it isn't the biggest fish or the most that wins, it's the teams with the highest weight. Every fish *must* be alive or their weight doesn't count."

We were in our boat by 6:00 a.m., rechecking equipment and bait. When the bell rang at 7:00, motors started. Every boat was trying to get out at once, so it took a while. We headed to the spot we picked the night before. Once settled, I took a deep breath. My dream of participating in a walleye tournament was happening.

Neither of us had a bite in the first hour, so we moved our boat. Soon, Kegan had one on the line and reeled it in slowly. It measured 19 inches, a keeper. I thought, *now it's my turn*. That's when Kegan's rod started tapping. He had another on the line. The walleye he reeled in looked small. But it was 14.1 inches. We had found our spot. I felt the *tap-tap-tap* on my line. This was my time. Pulling the rod hard to the left and feeling the pull, I knew I had him. Reeling it in slowly, Kegan's net brought it into the boat. This one measured 16.5 inches. Over the next few hours, we caught three more keepers and had to toss two back. Too small! I kept checking the live well to make sure all were alive. Those babies weren't going to die on my watch. With two hours left, I kept eyeing other anglers who were catching fish. I was anxious.

During the next hour we had a few nibbles. Kegan asked if I wanted to move. "Let's wait another ten minutes," I answered. That's when I felt the taps. Taking a deep breath, holding my rod, I pulled hard. My rod bent so I knew it was a big one. I wasn't going to let my go line slack and lose this one. Keeping my line tight, giving it just enough play, I reeled it in. This was big. My arms were tired. Kegan was ready with his net. When he saw it, he just said, "F...uck, That's huge!" When he measured, it was 26.2 inches! The tournament was ending. Time to go in.

Waiting for our fish to be weighed, I was pacing. "Kegan, how much could we win?" I asked. "Anything from nothing to $6,000," Kegan said.

Our fish totaled 24.7 pounds. It took another 40 minutes to complete all the weigh-ins. The announcer began reading names starting with eighth place. At second place the announcer called our names. I screamed! "We won $4,000!" Unexpectedly, Kegan wrapped me in his arms, and kissed me. Wow! I thought, maybe I've just won more than my first fishing tournament.

Inspired by the teachings of her Native American grandmother, Colleen Baldrica began her spiritual journey and her love for nature as a child. Today, Colleen is a retired educator, a presenter and the author of *Tree Spirited Woman.* Her mission: "Encourage and inspire women wherever they are in their life journey." web: treespiritedwoman.com

The Gambler

Gloria Fredkove

"Hello, I'm Rebecca." George's new therapist shook his hand firmly. "Have a seat." He sat down on the black leather chair, cleared his throat and said, "Nice place you have here."

She turned towards him, smiled, and said, "So, George? What can I help you with?"

"Well, can you lend me a few dollars?" Rebecca looked confused. Was this a joke? "I'm sorry, I don't carry checks or cash with me," she said.

"I'm just kidding. Anyway, I'm here because I can't sleep at night and eat junk food all day long."

"Your primary care doctor said you were depressed and feeling some anxiety."

"Well, Rebecca, I don't feel anxious right now, because you have an amazingly calming effect on me. Did anyone ever tell you that you have the most beautiful brown eyes? And not only that, but they go perfectly with your long, shiny brown hair."

"Thank you. Let's get back to you." George thought he saw her blush.

"Well, Dr. French thinks I'm depressed, but that's okay. I don't pay much attention to problems. I like to look at the beauty in life."

"Do you live alone?"

"Yes."

"What's that like?"

"Well, let's put it this way—if I had a choice, I'd rather live anywhere else. No one speaks English in the building, and they all use walkers or wheelchairs. It's depressing. Every other day there's an ambulance there, taking someone to the hospital. And you know what? Sometimes they don't come back. People there are just waiting to die. I'd like to live with people who haven't given up on life."

Rebecca Hauser was 60 years old. Married at one time, and had now been single for close to 20 years. She loved her career as a therapist. She considered herself an excellent listener, but staying neutral was hard for her. When Rebecca wasn't working as a therapist, she volunteered as a piano accompanist for senior citizens at *Well Care*, when they gathered in the library/music room for weekly sing-alongs.

As she studied George, things didn't add up. He was getting Medicaid, yet he looked like he shopped at Nordstrom. He appeared to be in his late 60s or early 70s, yet he was 80 years old. Rebecca wondered how he could be living in HUD housing, dressed in expensive clothes and shoes.

George had always had a great sense of style. In his younger years, he made lots of money selling everything from encyclopedias to frozen meat. None of the jobs lasted more than a few months. When he left New York for Texas, he sold used cars. As soon as he got paid, practically his entire earnings were spent at the racetrack. Still, he only bought expensive, well-made shirts and stylish jackets. But these days, all he could afford was thrift stores and consignment shops. George could smell a good deal before he even walked into the store. His ex-wife, Lydia, who made a great salary as a program manager, helped him out now and then with cash that she sent via Western Union. She also had a great eye for fashion.

"So, George, you said you don't like where you're living. What else is going on?"

"Well, I should have followed my dreams when I had the chance—when I was young." George looked around the office and stopped at a picture of elephants. Then, he returned her gaze. Suddenly, he started to sing, *"I'm in the mood for love, simply because you're near me. Funny but when you're near me, I'm in the mood for love."*

Rebecca blushed. "You have a lovely voice, George. Did you sing professionally?" She seemed so happy to hear him sing that he wanted to keep singing.

"No, I sing because I like to make people happy. I sing all the time. I sing on the bus, I sing at the doctor's office, I sing in the street."

"I'm glad to hear that. Music has been a part of my life since I was a young girl."

"Hey, you sound like you appreciate good music," George said, with a broad smile. He began scratching the sparse amount of white hair left on his mostly bald head. It seemed to relax him.

"I like all kinds of music, but I *love* classical music."

"My sister loves classical music. Personally, I love jazz. Nothing relaxes me more than a good CD of Miles Davis, Dave Brubeck, or Duke Ellington—guys from that era. They were the best! I grew up in New York and saw them perform in person."

"I see that you're divorced. How long ago did that happen?"

"Well, it was mostly my fault. I was married to the most beautiful, loving woman in the world, but I was a lousy provider. She made the money for both of us while I threw it away at the racetrack."

"I see. And how long have you gambled?"

"All my life."

George looked at Rebecca, waiting for her to say something. She waited for him to continue. He finally broke the silence.

"I spent all my time at the racetrack. I love horses, love to see them run. They're beautiful animals. I ... I was so stupid. I should have quit when I could, but I just kept right on going until all my money was gone and my wives left me."

"How many times were you married?"

"I lost count, but I think it was five times."

"Do you have children?"

"I have a daughter, Judy, from my most recent marriage. She's 25 years old. She's smart and beautiful, and I love her with all my heart. I wish I could have been a better father to her." George brushed away a tear.

"Just one daughter?"

"Well, I have—or I should say, I had a son, but I haven't heard from him in a long time. I'd rather not go into that right now."

"That's fine, George. This session is for you. How can I help you right now?"

"To be honest with you, Rebecca, I don't believe in therapy. My doctor told me to come to see you, so here I am. I believe in God. God has protected me so far, so I must be doing something right. I mean, doesn't that make sense?" George scratched his head.

Now Rebecca found herself distracted. Was it the way George said her name? *Rebecca.* It sounded like the most beautiful name in the world when he said it. She tried to regain her composure.

"I do believe that religion and spirituality help a lot of people cope with life's challenges. Tell me, what was your childhood like?"

"My father died when I was three years old. I don't remember him. My mother was sick for as long as I can remember."

"I'm sorry."

George took a deep breath and exhaled as if he was about to release the weight of the world. "My mother had a bad heart, she was depressed, and she couldn't work. She had asthma and, in those days, they didn't have good drugs for that."

"It sounds so hard for a young child to go through life with only one parent, and then to have that parent be sick."

"My sister had it rough, too. Our mother was always yelling, always critical, always upset about something. Susan cleaned, cooked, and took care of our mother after her heart attack. She became the adult. And where was I all that time? Gambling. I tried to stop, but I couldn't."

"Have you ever been in treatment for your gambling addiction?"

"No. I just kept trying to stay away, but I couldn't. I made the racetrack rich."

"And I see that you quit high school in the ninth grade?"

"I hated school. I couldn't learn to read, and the kids kept bullying me. I had a "big nose." My "feet smelled like bad cheese." They always found some new way of ridiculing me. So, I decided to quit and make some money on the street, selling ice cream. I was pretty good, too. But then I got involved in a gang, and we beat up on other kids. I was getting back at them for those kids that bullied me."

"Are you carrying around some guilt or shame about that?"

George crossed his leg over his knee and started swinging it back and forth.

"Did it make you feel like you were different from everyone else?"

"I *was* different." George scratched his head again. "Listen, I'd like to talk about something other than my childhood. Maybe we can talk about how I can't get to sleep at night. Would that be okay with you?"

"Sure. Tell me about that."

George fidgeted for a minute, without answering. He then started to sing, *"I'm in the mood for love ...."*

Rebecca thought he had a beautiful voice and didn't want him to stop. But he quit singing after just the first line. She was hoping George would open up a little more. After a few minutes, he continued.

"You know, I don't like to revisit the past. I live in the present. I never had sleeping issues until about five years ago when I moved to Minnesota. Maybe I should have stayed in Texas. My former wife is there, and so is my daughter. And I miss them every single day."

"Can't you move back?"

"Not without a job. I've been looking for work since I got here, but there aren't too many people hiring 80-year-olds."

"You have a beautiful voice, George. Have you considered singing as a way to make some money?"

"Unfortunately, I can't remember the words to the songs. And I can't stand on my feet very long. I take the bus to get groceries, and I can't believe how damn cold it is here in Minnesota! Sometimes I can't feel my toes. But my sister's here, and she gives me a small allowance every month. And the health care system here is a hundred times better than anywhere else I've lived. Maybe if I had someone in my life, I wouldn't complain about the weather."

"George, are you still gambling?"

"No. I haven't gambled since I got to Minnesota."

"Is that why you're getting financial aid?"

"No, I'm getting financial aid because my social security check is barely enough for food. Are you warm? It feels really warm in here."

"I actually feel a little cold. It's January."

"I understand. It's just that in my apartment, they keep the temperature at 80 degrees. I burn up. And it's starting to feel like that in here."

"I'm sorry. Would you like some cold water?"

"That would be awesome!"

Rebecca got up from her chair and opened the door behind her. She took a bottle of chilled water from a mini-fridge inside, and handed it to George. He gulped it down quickly.

"Now, that hit the spot. How much do I owe you?"

"It's on the house."

George stared at the picture of the elephants. Finally, he said, "That picture of the elephants?"

"Yes. What about it?"

"It's the most beautiful picture I've seen in a long time. I love animals. I would have to say that dogs are my favorite. Especially golden retrievers. Their eyes are so expressive."

"I love dogs, too. George, we're approaching the end of our time for today. I hope you'll come back. You've had a lot of challenges in your life, and I'd like to help you with your present challenges. If you're willing, we could get you some antidepressants and something for the anxiety. It will make a big difference."

"So, when do I come back?"

"Let's make an appointment for a week from today. Does that work for you?"

"Perfect."

"Okay, I'll see you next Thursday, at 2:00 p.m."

"Before I go, Rebecca, can I ask you something?"

"Sure."

"Are you single?"

"Yes, I am, why do you ask?"

"Because I would love to take you to a jazz club in downtown Minneapolis. It's called The Dakota. My sister's taken me there a few times, and they've got the best jazz."

"Well, I'd love to do that, but we have a relationship as therapist and client, and it wouldn't be ethical."

"Why not? We're not getting married, we're just friends."

"Sorry, I have to decline your sweet offer."

George shuffled into Rebecca's office for his eighth appointment. He looked downtrodden and like he hadn't slept in days.

"Hi, George, you look exhausted. Is everything okay?"

"Not really."

"What's going on?"

"Well, I've been coming here for a couple of months now, and you know all about me. But I don't know anything about you."

"Well, you don't need to know anything about me, George. These sessions are for you. I explained that to you."

"I realize that, but I care about you. You know about my pain, now I want to know about yours. I'm sure you've had some challenges in your life, haven't you?"

"Everyone has."

"I don't care about everyone. I care about you, Rebecca. I want to know about your life. Did you have a happy childhood?"

"It wouldn't be appropriate for me to discuss my life with you, George. This therapy is for you."

"I think you're scared to tell me about yourself. You're hiding behind your professional title. But I can tell you're in pain." George got up and walked right up to Rebecca. He bent down and looked into her eyes.

"Tell me, Rebecca, do you feel nothing when I look into those soulful eyes? Because eyes tell us more than words do, and yours look sad right now."

George gently lifted Rebecca's chin and kissed her softly on the lips. To his surprise, she didn't pull away.

"There. That wasn't so terrible, was it?"

Rebecca took a deep breath. She could feel that she was flushed, and she paused while planning what to say. "George, please, sit down. I can't see you again. I'm flattered, but this is not okay."

"You're breaking up with me after our first kiss? Was it that bad?"

"No, it was nice, actually. What I mean is, I can no longer be your therapist. We've just crossed a professional boundary."

"I'm sorry. But the truth is, if I had to choose between you being my therapist or being someone that I can have as a friend, you know which I'd choose, don't you?"

"You're old enough to be my father, George."

"That may be, but I'm a kid at heart, and so are you."

"I'm not a kid at heart."

"You most certainly are. You've got big puppy eyes, and you're beautiful. Listen, you know I don't have much money, and I can't drive right now. I had a minor car accident about a year ago, and my car was a total loss. But I'd like to get to know you better. The antidepressants I'm taking are working great. Most nights I sleep like a baby. My former wife just sent me some money, and I want to take you to The Dakota. Will you allow me that?"

"Well ... as long as we're clear that we are no longer therapist and client."

George nodded. "Rebecca, I'm assuming you have a car?"

"Of course."

"Perfect. Can you pick me up at my apartment building at 6:00 tomorrow night? We'll have dinner first and then see the show."

"My head is telling me this is not a good thing, George."

"What is your heart telling you?"

"That's the problem. I'm fascinated by you, but I'm not ready for romance."

"Let's not worry about that right now. Life is too short."

"George, we have to have an exit interview since you'll have to see someone else if you want to continue with your therapy."

"I'm not going to see anyone else. I feel better than I have in a very long time."

"That's good to hear. I have a few questions to ask you, if you don't mind?"

"Not at all."

"Have you found the therapy helpful?"

"Definitely."

"How has it helped you?"

"Well, I think just telling you about my life and my problems with gambling has been good for me. I'm sleeping better, and I don't need as many naps during the day."

"That's great. How's the eating issue coming along? Are you attending Overeaters Anonymous?"

"No, I'm just cutting back on bread and pasta. Those are my problem foods. I've never been that interested in sweets."

"Okay, but please keep in mind that there are programs for eating disorders and if you find that it's getting out of control again, I want you to reach out to someone."

"I'll keep that in mind."

One last question. Is there anything that you needed and did not receive in these sessions? In other words, do you have any complaints?

"No complaints. You've been terrific."

<hr>

A few weeks later, Rebecca and George went to The Dakota. They had a great time and George made her laugh. They became close friends. One night, Rebecca was waiting to pick him up to go back to The Dakota. She waited for 15 minutes, then called him on the phone, but it went to voicemail. She was worried.

As she parked her car, she noticed that paramedics were bringing someone out on a stretcher. Rebecca glanced over and saw that it was George. He was white as a ghost, and his eyes were closed. She sat in her car and prayed. She followed the ambulance to the emergency room at Methodist Hospital. As the paramedics guided the stretcher out of the ambulance, she saw that George's face was covered. Her worst fear had come true.

After the funeral, Rebecca went to The Dakota, cried her eyes out, and felt the power of jazz like never before.

Gloria Fredkove has taken many writing classes at The Loft. In 2009 she wrote and directed a play, *Snow in the City*, which was performed by Parlor Players. Her poems have been published in *Writers in the Know* (WINK). She is a member of Women of Words (WOW) and thanks them for their encouragement, which led to two stories being published in this anthology. Gloria is writing a memoir about her childhood, *Casual Baggage*. Special thanks to husband, Joe, for his support of all of Gloria's creative endeavors, including her choral memberships in Minnesota Chorale and Singers in Accord.

Here Kitty, Kitty...

CONNIE ANDERSON

After dark one day my human said, "Silky, come on, we're going for a ride," as he sort of playfully took off my collar and put it on the counter.

Once in the car, I look at Bob from my perch on the passenger seat, and meow loudly, but he doesn't look at me. After about a ten-minute drive, he pulls over to the curb and drops me out on the grass. I look at him as he drives away—but he doesn't turn around.

After a few minutes of "cat"-astrophic thinking, I realized I had been dumped and left to survive on my own. Nothing looked familiar so I started walking—but I didn't know where.

That evening I spent under a bush, listening to my stomach telling me how hungry it was. I'm more of a house cat so scrounging for food did not come naturally to me. I found some garbage nearby and ate the remains of a couple burgers.

The next day I started looking around and came up to a big building in a very nice Minnesota neighborhood—at least it was big to me. It was fascinating, all the activity as cars went into a garage door, and cars came out a different garage door. I observed how the car stopped, the big door would open up, they drove in, and the door went down.

Hmmm, there was plenty of time for someone like me to sidle next to the car, and sneak in. I was looking for a place to sleep, be away from weather, and feel safe. I could run around outside all day after escaping next to a car leaving and sneak back in with the next car at the other door.

This is what I did day in and day out without being seen. Then one day I must have been careless, and I hear a woman yelling, "Ralph, I think I just saw a cat in here!"

One of my hiding places was on top of the tire where I could safely rest without being easily seen. With about 200 cars, I had a lot of tires to move around to.

———————— ❖ ————————

A couple weeks later I was spotted again by a woman who did not give up so easily. She was either a cat lover and wanted to help me—or she hated cats. Now I had to be quieter, quicker and smarter since I was not sure what my fate would be if I was caught.

As winter came, I was indoors more, and happily had discovered the building's garbage room was filled with lots of good smells. Why hadn't I found it earlier?

I had learned to listen for human voices and footsteps. One day mid-December something new appeared by the garbage bin. It was a strange metal contraption that looked like if you got into it, you would never get out. The next day

I found food inside it, obviously placed there by someone who knows a cat's palate and what they like to eat.

On top of everything, I wasn't feeling very good. I'm a girl cat, or so a boy cat told me on one of our evening meet-ups this fall.

Wham! What a sound as the trap door slams down making me a prisoner. I was not one bit happy.

However, the woman who brought the trap was thrilled, a relief to me as she was obviously a cat lover.

The lady took me to her apartment on the fourth floor and groomed me. I had really missed being petted so I was feeling pretty good.

Then came her great reveal: "Look, this cat is pregnant—and I think the kittens are coming soon."

I could not believe my good luck as this woman was a volunteer at the humane society. She helped me have my five kittens. Then she found a new home for me as well as for each of the kittens.

Actually, my new home was with her so when she calls, "Here kitty, kitty," now I come running. Wouldn't you?

Connie Anderson edits books and has written four books: *In My Next Life, I Want to be My Dog, When Polio Came Home: How Ordinary People Overcame Extraordinary Challenges, Man Overboard: Hubby's Getting a New Boat,* and *The 'I' of a Woman.*

www.WordsandDeedsInc.com

Home Sweet Home

KATHI HOLMES

P eering out the window, all she saw were old people planted in the green webbed aluminum lawn chairs. A tree stood bare. It had died before it had a chance to grow. A mix of sadness and anger swirled in her mind.

I don't want to be here. How did I end up in this place?

Her life had always been ordinary and respectable. She had four grown children and five lovely grandchildren. Mark, her oldest son, and his wife had gotten her into this mess.

Her husband Marvin passed away after 43 years of marriage. They said it looked like suicide.

"I don't believe it," she had insisted. "Marvin was a strong, German man. Those types of people don't commit suicide even if they make bad decisions."

Money was tight when they first got married. It wasn't long before Marvin was making a substantial income as a mechanic. After the kids were all in school Alice took a part-time secretarial job to help pay for their college. They lived comfortably, but Marvin wanted more.

"We should have money to travel when we retire. Enjoy life." That made him ripe for an invitation to invest in a risky, but seemingly fruitful venture.

While having breakfast with his friend Joe, he found himself listening intently to Joe's story about the great earnings he had with the Bernard C. Mavik Investment Securities firm. Marvin couldn't wait to relay the information to Alice. The business was one of the top Wall Street investment firms. "We can't go wrong," insisted Marvin. Neither Marvin nor Alice understood much about the stock market, but the firm had been in business for forty years, so Alice agreed to make a small investment. What she didn't know was that Marvin continued to invest more and more of their savings into Bernie Mavik's firm. He took out a second mortgage on the house. After all, the statements were impressive.

When Marvin heard that Bernie Mavik was being accused of conducting a Ponzi scheme, he didn't understand what that was. Then he found out that they had lost all of their savings. Alice wanted to know what happened, but Marvin wouldn't talk about it. When he came home from work, he just sat in his recliner and blankly stared at the television. This routine continued for months until the day he saw Bernie Mavik on the television screen handcuffed and on his way to prison. The next day Marv "accidently" took too many sleeping pills—and left Alice to pick up the pieces.

"How could he have done that? Invested all our money and mortgaged the house too," Alice told the kids after the funeral.

The bills started piling up, and the bank kept calling, requesting payment on the mortgage and threatening foreclosure. Mark started to investigate alternative living arrangements.

"I don't want to move."

"Mom, you can't live here. You can't afford it. We have to find you a place where you don't have to worry about money and all the bills."

"I don't like any of these places you are showing me."

"You can't live here. You don't have the money. It's just not there."

Morningside Senior Community was now her new home. She hated it. She didn't want to play Bingo or watch movies with those old people. Her apartment was just a box with three rooms and a small kitchen.

The last straw was when Mark dropped off a cute little Cairn terrier puppy he had adopted from the local humane society. After unpacking all the dog paraphernalia and explaining what needed to be done to take care of the dog, he left.

Alice stared at the dog. "What am I going to do with you?" That was all the encouragement the dog needed to jump up on her lap, stare in her face with wanting eyes and frantically lick her cheek.

The dog had come with the name Bernie, but that would never do. So, Alice named him Charlie. She reaffirmed to herself that doing so did not mean he was going to stay.

"Now I suppose you want to go outside, Charlie?"

With the leash adjusted securely, but not too tight, Alice took off with Charlie. Not having gone outside since she moved in, she did not realize what a beautiful day awaited them. They followed the path through the woods. Charlie was a little slow and liked to sniff every leaf and crevice. That was okay. Alice had a chance to observe the scenery.

A week went by before Mark called his mother. "How is the dog working out?"

"His name is Charlie. He's not staying, you know."

The conversation was short because Alice had to take Charlie out for a walk.

A neighbor, Joan, had an apricot poodle who Charlie loved to play with. One day she invited Joan to come for coffee and bring Issy. Alice found that she and Joan had many things in common. They were both widows. Joan lived with her alcoholic husband until he died, leaving her with little money to live on. They were both disappointed at having to move to Morningside. Joan, however, had found other friends in the building and around the neighborhood. She had become quite happy with the living arrangements.

Charlie had a gregarious and enthusiastic demeanor and couldn't pass up introducing himself to other dogs. At first Alice was embarrassed but she realized it was a great way to meet new friends. She began to have regular conversations with other dog owners and shared dog stories and tips. She was invited to join a bridge club by another dog owner in a neighboring building. Charlie was a good companion and wanted to go with her wherever she went. Lunches, concerts and movies kept her so busy she needed to keep track of it all on the calendar of her new iPad which the gentleman down the hall had taught her how to use. Bingo was even fun because she found herself laughing more than she had in years.

Alice found a new life that was of her making and she loved it. She had a companion who barked a little, but he didn't complain. And he loved her unconditionally—especially the treats she couldn't resist giving him.

She did feel a little guilty when she had to turn down a visit from her kids because she was too busy. Alice and Charlie had not just found a home. They had found a community.

She now had that enjoyable life she and Marvin had dreamed of.

Kathryn M. Holmes has published four books, *I Stand with Courage: One Woman's Journey to Conquer Paralysis,* the story of her recovery from a below the waist paralysis. *Reflections,* a self-published book providing bits of wisdom and reflection on family, friends, dating, marriage, society, the workplace, grandchildren and aging. *Watershed Moments,* stories from men and women who experienced life challenges. After the death of her husband, she compiled *Thoughts and Prayers for those Experiencing Loss.* These books can be found on Amazon.com. She lives in Minnetonka, Minnesota with her dog, Honey.

The Horse

KAREN ENGSTROM ANDERSON

The year was 1927, and the two young men had decided to seek their fortunes in the United States. They had read the flyers posted at the railroad station, touting the abundance of jobs and opportunities they'd find there.

As Helmer and Anders stepped onto the Swedish American Lines ship, they were excited to see what lay ahead. Onboard, they met two farmers returning to the United States after having visited their families. Mr. Vistad offered Helmer a job on his farm in Iowa. The other Swede, Mr. Peterson, said Anders should come with him to Minnesota, where he would help him find a job, but he couldn't stay with him because he already had a hired hand. The four of them traveled to Chicago, where the two young friends said goodbye with promises to meet in a year.

Peterson's farm was close to the South Dakota border, the land so flat, Anders thought he could see forever in every direction. Mr. Peterson learned about a farmer not too far away who needed help, so a few days later Anders headed west down the road, suitcase in hand.

After several hours he walked up a dirt path to a small clapboard house to ask for directions. It was in disrepair and looked sad to him, like no one cared about it. *I wonder who lives here?* He knocked on the door.

"Hello? Come in."

He stepped inside and saw an old woman at the stove. "Hello. Can you tell me the way to Lidberg's? I'm Anders, their new hired hand."

She stared at him in a strange way. "This is Lidberg's farm," she said and gave the handsome young man with wavy red hair an awkward, unwelcome hug.

She gave him a bowl of what she had been stirring. He nodded his thanks and ate. *I wonder what this is? Beans or maybe meat. Just eat it. It won't kill you.* It wasn't long before a big, gray-haired man walked in.

"This is our new farmhand. His name is Anders," Mrs. Lidberg said.

Anders stood to shake hands, but Mr. Lidberg just stared at him and then sat down to eat. *What an uncouth man.* When Lidberg finished eating, he leaned back.

"So, Anders, where did you come from, and why would you want to come here?"

Anders smiled and replied, "They say we can make a fortune here in the U.S. There are advertisements everywhere back home in Sweden telling us to come. And, besides, I didn't want to go into the Army, which I would have to do when I turn 18 next year."

"A coward, then, eh?" Lidberg said, getting up abruptly. "Come. I'll show you where you sleep." Anders started to follow him into a side room, but Lidberg came right out carrying a blanket and went to the door. Anders looked confused.

"That's my son's room. You can't sleep in there," the old man said.

Anders picked up his suitcase and followed his new boss outside. The small barn had two stalls; one housed a magnificent draft horse who eyed the stranger with interest, the other held several sheep. Mr. Lidberg gestured to the ladder and said, "The best place to sleep is up there. Here's a blanket. Be up at dawn and ready to work. Come to the house for food. Okay?"

Suddenly he realized he was being told to sleep in the barn with the animals. *What? I'm supposed to sleep in the barn? On a pile of straw? With no sheets or pillow? Where can I hang my clothes? Where can I brush my teeth? A bath! Where can I take a bath? He didn't even give me a towel! Who's going to wash my clothes? What other awful food will there be? I'm hungry already.* It was then he realized everything had changed. This was his new reality.

He wanted to leave right then, but he had committed to working through the harvest, so he said, "Okay."

That first night was endless. The noises of the animals, the smells, and the loneliness. Finally, sleep came, then immediately it was dawn. He got up and went to the hand pump in the yard. He swept back his hair with wet hands, splashed his face with the frigid water, and filled his canteen.

After breakfast, the two men went to the barn.

"Do you ride?" asked Lidberg.

Anders shook his head. He had never ridden a horse. Back home, there were plow horses, of course, but no one ever rode them. They had cars, trains, motorcycles, and boats. Why would they ride a horse?

"Okay. Pay attention then," said Lidberg as he put the bridle on the big gelding. Then he held the reins and a chunk of mane and nimbly flung himself onto the horse's bare back.

He slid off and handed the reins to Anders. "Okay, you do it now."

Anders took the reins and held them as Lidberg had. The horse was huge. Lidberg was huge. Anders mentally calculated what he needed to do and adjusted his approach. When he launched, all three of them stopped breathing—until he landed on his butt on the other side of the horse.

Lidberg let out a guffaw so loud that the horse bolted. He couldn't stop laughing, so Anders dusted himself off and went to retrieve the horse, now quietly eating grass on the shady side of the barn. *Son of a gun horse! I hate you. I hate Lidberg. I hate this place. I just want to go home. That old man did that on purpose. Nobody could ride that monster without a saddle!"*

Over the following weeks, Lidberg showed Anders how to do what was needed. He constantly grumped at the young man, but Anders learned quickly and didn't mind hard work. Even so, Lidberg had no kind words for Anders, who counted the days until he could leave.

Lidberg's farm was 2,080 acres of flat land, barren of trees and most brush. Anders found himself almost more homesick for trees than he was for his family. One of his jobs was repairing the barbed-wire fencing. He mastered how to saddle the horse, pack the saddlebags with tools, and strap the canvas-wrapped roll of wire and a couple of poles over the horse's haunches. While Anders worked, the horse was tied to the fence so there would be easy access to the supplies and tools.

One day in July, Mr. Lidberg told Anders to take the horse into town on an errand. Anders was excited to have a little time to spend on his own. At the mercantile, he found a wide-brimmed straw hat which would be better to wear in the heat than the felt hat he brought from Sweden. A bright-colored tie caught his eye, and he bought that, too. Looking in the mirror, he tied it the way his father had taught him. *This tie is so good-looking, even Elsa would flirt with me.*

A fierce wind had come up while he was in town, and Anders had to hold the brim of his new hat as he rode back to the farm. The blowing dust made him sneeze, and in that second, he took his hand off the brim of his hat. WHOOSH! and the hat blew away. *My new hat! We gotta catch it. Come on, you lazy horse! Hurry up!*

Anders kicked and kicked, and finally the big horse picked up his pace enough, so they caught up with the hat. There was a brief respite in the wind, and the hat lay still, upside down for just a moment. Anders got down to retrieve it and saw the horse holding it in his mouth. He snatched the hat away, tearing it into two pieces. The horse chewed the big chunk of brim while Anders swore.

I guess I shouldn't be mad. It was made of straw, after all. I hope it tasted good. When Anders tried to put his foot in the stirrup, the big horse side-stepped, making Anders lose his balance. Every time Anders attempted to mount, the horse would move a little. Anders tried everything. He yanked on the reins. He hollered in Swedish. He smacked the horse's withers. But nothing worked. *And I was just thinking I shouldn't be mad at you!* There was nothing to be done—so he had to walk home leading the horse. Lidberg laughed when they got there. *Darn horse. Darn grumpy old man. I can't wait to be far away from here.*

At supper, Mrs. Lidberg asked Anders, "What's that, eh?" pointing at his neck.

Anders touched his collar, then the knot of his new tie. He looked down, and his face froze in horror when he saw that the knot and a few long threads were all that was left of it. The rest had disintegrated in the wind. *I think I'll just give up. This day was a disaster.*

Mrs. Lidberg patted his arm and said, "You'll get another one."

"Thanks," he said and gave her a slight smile.

As Anders was leaving to go to sleep, Lidberg said, "You know, Anders, the horse is smart, and if he likes you, he'll let you mount him."

Maybe the old man is right. If he's smart, maybe the horse was just holding my hat so it wouldn't blow away. I shouldn't have been so mean to him. He grabbed a fistful of grass on the way to the barn and stopped at the horse's stall to give it to him. He rubbed his muzzle, and the horse nickered.

The next day, he set out to check the farthest fence line. It was the hottest day yet, with not a cloud in the sky. He was feeling strange when he stopped to have his lunch and realized he had forgotten to fill his canteen. *No water and I'm so thirsty! I really don't feel good. I wonder if I could die out here. I'd better get going.* He packed up, mounted the horse, and headed in the direction of the farm. But the horse kept fighting the reins. The relentless sun was almost directly overhead, and Anders began to doubt himself. *Am I going in the right direction? What's this darn horse doing? If he keeps pulling in the same direction, doesn't he know we'll be going in a circle? A circle! I really could die out here!*

The horse kept going in the wrong direction. Anders felt so groggy that he finally gave up and just closed his eyes. Suddenly he was thrown forward—almost out of the saddle. *What is going on? Where am I?* He pulled himself up straight as the horse went down a short but very steep incline. At the bottom was a small mud puddle surrounded by hoof prints and a few low bushes. The horse stopped and pawed the ground until a small pool of muddy water accumulated, which he drank. He repeated the process a couple of times and then stood still.

What do I do now? If I don't drink the mud, I could die. But if I drink it, I could die. If I get off the darn horse, he won't let me on again, and I could die. What should I do?

The horse stood with his head down, almost as if he was sleeping. Thirst finally prevailed, and Anders got off the horse. On his knees, he began to dig, making a hole for the water to accumulate. He put his lips to the liquid and drank as much as he could, then he lay back. When he awoke, he was in the shade of the horse. *I'm going to make it. It's lucky the horse moved so I was out of the sun, or I'd really be cooked. I'd better start back.*

Anders took the reins and prepared to mount. The horse turned his head to look at Anders. *Oh, no. He's getting ready to play his games. I'll never get on.* But when he put his foot in the stirrup, the horse stayed still and let him throw his other leg over. *Thank you, big fellow.* Anders gave him a pat, then another couple pats, and then some more. He didn't even realize he was crying until he reached up to brush at the tears dripping from his chin.

When they got back to the farm, Lidberg was standing there. He took the horse into the barn after Anders dismounted. Anders went to the pump and drank and splashed water on his face and head again and again. When he looked up, Lidberg was standing there.

"Come inside," the old man said.

Mrs. Lidberg looked concerned as she set a bowl of food in front of Anders. *Uh, oh. I must be in trouble. That's why he isn't talking to me.* Lidberg didn't speak until Anders had taken a few bites.

"You had a close call today, young man."

"I know," said Anders with a catch in his throat. "The horse saved me. But how did you know?"

"You always leave the pump handle down when you fill your canteen. Today the pump handle was up, as it should be. We were worried."

"I'm sorry," said Anders, relieved.

Anders began to realize that Lidberg had a kind side to him. They got along better, and the harvest went well. It was soon time for Anders to leave. The old man asked Anders to repair the last stretch of fencing before he left.

The next day, just after he had finished the repairs and was packing up, Anders heard the thundering of cattle hooves. *The horse! I have to untie him!* The horse was trying to free himself, yanking on the reins, snorting, and rearing. The herd, coming fast, had seen the fence and began to swerve away, but a few of the cattle couldn't avoid hitting the horse, forcing him into the barbed wire. Anders barely had time to roll under the fence to safety. Then they were gone, and the thunder subsided. The horse had managed to stay standing but was badly injured. A huge section of his chest hung loose and bloody. He stood very still as Anders looked him over. *Oh, my poor fellow.*

Anders got the tools and the bag of wire, cut strips of canvas and took off his shirt. He closed the wound and pressed his folded shirt against it. Then he ran the canvas strips around the horse's chest at different angles and tied them to the saddle to hold the makeshift bandage in place. Hoping it would stay on, he coaxed the horse to take steps, and they started walking home.

As they got close, Anders hollered for Lidberg to come.

"I'm so sorry," said Anders. "The herd came at us fast."

"Let's have a look at him," Lidberg said. "You did a good job bandaging him up. How did you even think to do that?"

"I saw much worse when I worked at the sawmill back home. Except there, the injured guy got some akvavit to ease the pain."

Lidberg used a carpet needle and thick thread to sew the flesh into place. The horse barely moved. They held the water bucket to his muzzle and tried to feed him some oats, but he wouldn't drink or eat.

"We'll just have to wait and see," said the old man.

At supper, Lidberg said, "You'll be wanting to leave tomorrow, I expect."

"I'll stay another day if that's okay," said Anders.

That night he climbed down from the loft several times, trying to get the horse to drink, but he refused. Anders stayed close to the barn the next day to check on the horse. But he still wouldn't drink or eat. Before supper, Anders went into the stall again with a fresh bucket of water. *You're going to be all right. I just know it. Come on.*

Please take a drink. Look, it's really good water. Anders lifted the bucket to his face and pretended to drink. The horse raised his head a little. Anders offered the bucket to the horse, and he put his muzzle in and drank.

At supper, Anders said, "I think he's going to be good. Is it okay if I leave tomorrow?"

The old man looked at his wife, who reached over and put her hand on his. "Okay."

The next morning, Anders stood with the horse and rubbed his muzzle for a bit. *You get well now. They need you. I'm going to miss you, big fellow.* With tears in her eyes, Mrs. Lidberg hugged him. Mr. Lidberg walked with Anders to the gate. Anders turned to shake hands goodbye, but the old man just pulled him in for a rough hug. Their eyes met, but not a word was said. Anders turned and walked away. *I think I'm going to miss them, too.*

At the station, he walked around the room while he waited for the train. He stopped to look at the faded pictures of local men who had died in The Great War encased in a dusty glass case on the wall—young faces, eager and steadfast. Then he saw the photo of a young man who looked a lot like him, with the same thick wavy hair. He stared at the picture and at the name on the bottom—*Chuck Lidberg 1900-1917.* He thought about the choices he had made and the ones Chuck had made. *You should know how much your parents miss you. They are very proud of you. I'm so sorry I didn't get to meet you. You must have been a great guy just like your dad.*

On the train to Chicago, he looked out at the flat land, homesick still, and wondered what choices lay ahead for him.

Karen Engstrom Anderson writes historical fiction inspired by her father's stories. While translating his handwritten journals from Swedish, she became hooked on writing. She is working on a series of three books loosely based on his experiences. One of her short stories was included in *Minnesota Not So Nice: Eighteen Tales of Bad Behavior*.

I Have to Know...

CONNIE ANDERSON

Eighteen years ago in a small Minnesota town, Beth became pregnant late winter when she was 17. When she told her senior-year boyfriend, he started making plans—but it didn't include her or a baby. In fact, he escaped into the military the week he graduated.

Beth spent the rest of her junior year hiding her pregnancy from everyone, including herself. She tried not to think about *tomorrow*. When the summer break started, her parents drove her 60 miles to a home for unwed mothers and left her there alone to have a baby. The caregivers were wonderful, but both the baby—and the feeling of *extreme aloneness*—grew in her every day.

Beth decided—actually it was decided for her—that she was not going to mother her newborn baby. And from somewhere nearby, but so many heartbeats away, a grateful woman opened her arms in welcome, and became a most willing and able new mother.

With the certainty of a raindrop, Beth hoped that one day her birth daughter would want to know who and why— and so much more. She wanted to hug her and hold her close again because after her birth she had been allowed to hold her baby for only a few minutes.

Now almost two decades later, in another small town not far away, that baby had grown up. Throughout Judy's teen years, at every glance, the mirror reflected only her own solitary image, with no history showing in her eyes or hair, no same-nose or other features. No other faces looked back—not her birthmother, not grandmothers nor aunts. No hint of a father's eye color. No one ever said, "You look like your mom."

Judy had to trick herself into thinking of things that could be easily accomplished, so "Make *that first call!,*" always at the top of her to-do list, was followed by simple things, like "water my plants."

⸻ ⚹ ⸻

Now in her mid-thirties, a maturing Beth often woke from her dreams engulfed in deep sadness—with swirling memories of being a pregnant teenager; but then visions of her daughter with her other mother would prance through her dreams. In this dream, Beth was always on the outside looking in on their joyful life. Every year on her daughter's birthday she thought of her, hoping with all of her heart that she was happy.

The summer before she left for college at age 18, Judy's quests haunted her days and nights. *I want to know. I have to know.* Worrying how her parents would react, she asked her mom, who after taking a deep breath, told her she understood, and to go for it.

Facing her own fears, Beth now quietly admitted: *I want to know. I have to know, but...*

This slippery ice of searching can be unpredictably thin, so mother and daughter would have to step lightly, and be careful of each other's feeling as they seek the best path to the truth. Each one had her own idea of what that truth would look and feel like.

If this were a movie, the narrator would be saying: Judy knows her birthmother's name and finds it in the phone book. Now she is dialing, first, pushing the nine button; then the five. It's ringing. A woman answers...

But this wasn't fiction, and a woman's identity can disappear, usually by taking her new husband's name. Judy had done a lot of research into finding her birthmother. Some trails led her closer; others were painful and frustrating dead-ends.

On the other side, Beth knew if she was going on a search for this daughter of her memories, she had better pack a big lunch and take a change of underwear. Where the path would lead, no one knew.

Judy felt like a bridesmaid waiting for the bouquet toss. Both her youthful anticipation and trepidation were killing her. Will she lose something when this elusive woman is found, or will it be all win/win? Will they hug and have a good cry? Or...she couldn't even think about the *or*.

In her deep subconscious, Beth wondered: *Why am I making this about me?* The thought spun her around like she was on *Dancing with the Stars*, twirling and twirling, but not getting anywhere.

❧

Some days, Beth's incredible sadness was heartbreaking. *Would she ever lose that sense of loss and the forced abandonment of her child?* Beth's lightshow of guilt reminded her that maybe this young woman needed to know too, and she wished for only good things when they finally meet.

But now it was Judy's time—and her future, like soft clay, was waiting for her hands to mold it into her vision. She had eagerly passed the no-turning-back point, and a successful reunion seemed closer.

This search, this find, this connection, well, it would change their lives forever. Beth couldn't even talk to her husband about her butterflies of doubt, about closure and new beginnings, or about her dream. *Will the news be good—for everyone?* At that moment, she would have liked to trade her heart-to-stomach nervous worry, but...

Wait, the phone was ringing. Beth answers, not recognizing the name on caller ID. A young woman's voice spoke softly, asking. "Is this Beth Andrews from New Elms, Minnesota?"

Beth's voice waivered, saying "Yes," as her heart already knew what her mind would quickly realize. "Yes, yes. Is this who I hope it is?"

They talked about, laughed about, and shared the past many years in both their lives—enjoying the similarities in what they liked to do, read, eat, and watch. When they talked about their families on this first visit, Judy shared that she has a brother who is also adopted. Beth was forthright about her maternal pride in her son and daughter, and her good marriage.

With sadness mixed with joy, they finally hung up, but not before plans were made to talk again soon.

Now sitting at the kitchen table at home, Judy was a bit nervous because she would never want to hurt her mother, the woman who raised her. With her hand on her heart, her whispered words said it all: *"Mom, guess who I found?"*

Connie Anderson edits books and has written four books: *In My Next Life, I Want to be My Dog, When Polio Came Home: How Ordinary People Overcame Extraordinary Challenges, Man Overboard: Hubby's Getting a New Boat,* and *The 'I' of a Woman.*

www.WordsandDeedsInc.com

Lollie's Folly

MIDGE BUBANY

———— ✤ ————

Detective Fiona Winter opened the "Unsolved Homicides" file and briefed her trainee, Eddie Navarre.

"A decade ago on July 15, 2009, at approximately 0700 hours, forty-five-year-old Frederick Vonn was found deceased on his garage floor by his jogging partner. The Hennepin County medical examiner estimated the time of death between 2000 and 2300 hours, July 14. Cause of death was blunt-force trauma. His house was ransacked, and the victim's blood was found on a garden spade near his body and determined to be the murder weapon. Indicating what, Eddie?"

"They used what was handy. The murder was unplanned," he said.

"Bingo. Vonn was a widower and lived alone. He taught high school physical education and coached gymnastics. Also, there was a severe thunderstorm that evening, and the power went out around nine o'clock and wasn't restored until the next afternoon. That's probably why neighbors didn't notice anything suspicious."

"Suspects?"

"I met with Charlie Carlson, the lead detective, now retired. He had one suspect: Vonn's next-door neighbor, Arnold Purcell. A few neighbors had commented on the bad blood between the two men. Purcell was alone that night as his wife was visiting her mother in Redwood Falls, and his fourteen-year-old son, Thomas, was on a sleepover. Carlson said Purcell is a strange dude. He's an electrical engineer and, in his interview, he smirked when he said if he wanted to kill Vonn, he would have electrocuted him."

"Whoa."

"Carlson thought Purcell clever enough to stage a burglary or robbery. Someone spent time wiping prints off the spade and doorknobs. But without physical evidence or a confession, Purcell didn't have enough to make an arrest."

"Maybe he didn't kill him," Eddie said.

"Exactly. It's critical to be objective. All Vonn's associates and his other neighbors had alibis, so it could have been a random act. In that case, we have our work cut out for us. Let's take a drive to the Purcells."

Fiona parked on Blaisdell Avenue, narrowed from the recent snowfall. As she exited the unmarked Crown Vic, she pulled up her collar to fight the bone-chilling January wind. Steamy puffs of breath preceded the pair as they walked to the residence, snow underfoot crunching with each step on the not-yet-shoveled sidewalk.

Lollie Purcell dropped her *People* magazine in her lap when she noticed the black car pull up. A man and woman exited the car and walked toward her front door.

What did they want? Her heart thumped as she dropped to her knees and crawled along the wall to hide herself from view, thinking *Go Away!* When she didn't answer the doorbell, they resorted to pounding on the door several times.

"Police. Open up!" Detective Winter announced.

Cops! Lollie's heart sank. It was silly to hope it was over. But what exactly did they know? More pounding.

"We saw you in the window, ma'am. We know you're home."

Her breathing quickened. Dang it. They'd kick the door in if she didn't open it. *Okay, calm down, Lollie.* She stood, took three deep breaths, plastered a smile on her face, and opened the door. The woman in front of her was plain, sturdy but could be pretty if she fixed herself up. Behind her was a kid, not much older than Thomas. He had a crooked nose and the shoulders of a Viking's football player.

"Mrs. Purcell?" Detective Winter said.

Lollie blinked innocently. "Yes?"

"Detective Winter with the Minneapolis Police Department, and this is Investigator Navarre." They flashed badges. "We're re-investigating the murder of Frederick Vonn," the detective said.

Lollie stared at her.

The detective frowned and cocked her head. "He was your next-door neighbor on Garfield."

She cast a forlorn look and nodded. "Yes, poor Fred."

"May we come in?"

It would look bad if she refused, wouldn't it? "Yes, but I have to leave for a funeral shortly."

The pair kicked off their snowy boots, crossed the room in stocking feet, and sat on her sofa. Lollie took her chair by the window, leaned back, crossed a leg, and nonchalantly swung her foot. Then she had a thought and popped up.

"Would you care for a cup of coffee?"

"No, thanks," Detective Winter said, making Lollie sink back into her chair.

"When did you move here?"

"Nine years ago."

"Is Arnold home?"

"Um, no. He's ice fishing. Up north. Somewhere." As she pointed northward, Lollie noticed her hand was trembling, so she folded her hands and held them in her lap.

"When's he's returning?"

Lollie shrugged. "Not sure."

"Call his cell phone and ask."

"He doesn't have one because he says the government tracks us through our electronic devices."

"Who's he with?"

"No one."

Detective Winter narrowed her unbelieving eyes.

Lollie pointed in the air. "I have to leave in a few minutes. They're counting on my tater-tot hotdish, and I'm serving."

"Tater-tot hotdish? That's what smells so good," Navarre said, smiling.

Detective Winter leaned forward. "I'll be quick. Some of your former neighbors recalled a conflict your husband had with Mr. Vonn."

"Who said that?" Lollie asked. "Must have been the nosey ol' biddy, Bonnie Kleinschmidt."

"What was the problem?" the detective asked.

Lollie pulled her lips in a tight line. "It was so long ago I can't believe anyone even brought it up. Anyway, when the Twins were in the World Series, Fred won two tickets from a radio station and took me because I'm the biggest fan ever, which got some neighbor's panties in a bundle, and *that's* what upset Arnold and caused problems with Fred."

Navarre smiled. "I'm a die-hard fan too. Which World Series game did you attend with Mr. Vonn?"

"Game six in '91. They played the Atlanta Braves and went eleven innings. The Twins won four to three. Best day of my life." Lollie put a hand on her heart.

"I noticed the framed homer hanky you have on the wall above your desk," he said.

The detective cleared her throat and butted into their conversation. "Mrs. Purcell said she's in a hurry." She was sitting unladylike with her elbows resting on her thighs. "Ma'am, the falling out I was referring to occurred after a neighborhood intervention in which your neighbors, including Mr. Vonn, demanded your husband return all the tools and machines he borrowed."

Lollie's back straightened. "Intervention? Is that what Bonnie called it? She set up a fake party to blindside us. Such a nasty person."

"Did you return the items?"

"Except for the missing chainsaw." *Enough of this!* Lollie rose, pointed to her watch, and declared she had to leave for church.

"One more thing. How would you describe your relationship to the Vonns?"

"Arnold and Fred mostly avoided each other, and despite what Bonnie thought, Juliet and I remained close, very close. When she was dying from cancer, I was the one who brought meals and did all the housework. The *Christian* thing to do." Lollie sighed letting them know what a good person she was and how heartbreaking Juliet's death was to her. "Now, I really must go."

"Thank you for your time," the detective said. She placed a card on the coffee table, then stood. "Please have Mr. Purcell call the moment he returns."

When they approached the door, Detective Winter turned to ask: "You have one registered vehicle. How are you getting to the church if Mr. Purcell took it fishing?"

Her face grew hot. "He. . . didn't take the car."

"How did he get up north then?"

"I don't know. He just left a note while I was out, saying he went fishing and would be back in a week."

"Then how would you know if he went alone?"

"The note said so."

"May I see it?"

"No, I threw it away and the trash was picked up this morning."

"I see."

After the cops left, Lollie tossed the business card in the trash. She grabbed her hot dish out of the oven and put it in the carrier. She said good-bye to Arnold and told him they may have to move to Florida after all.

Mrs. Purcell pulled the 2009 silver Chevy Impala out of the garage, drove down the alley onto 46th Street, then turned right on Lyndale.

Following several car lengths behind, Fiona said, "I wonder what the church ladies will think of Lollie serving in her leopard print tunic, gold leggings, and faux snake-skin knee-high boots."

Eddie laughed. "Do you believe her story about Arnold's whereabouts?"

"Seemed fishy. Pardon the terrible pun."

"Ha! He could have rented a car or took a bus."

"His driver's license has expired. He'd need one to rent."

"Did he not renew because he lost his license?"

"Nothing on his record," Fiona said.

"Do you think he was home?"

"I don't know, but hiding would speak volumes. Funny how she thought the conflict was about Vonn taking her to a baseball game," Fiona said. "She knew her neighbors thought it was inappropriate."

"Makes me think Vonn and Lollie had something going on, and Arnold was jealous and killed him in a jealous rage."

"Possibly. Lollie's twenty-two years younger than her husband. According to file photos, Vonn was trim and handsome, but Arnold Purcell not so much. Hopefully, the years have increased Purcell's guilt and he needs to relieve his conscience."

"Boss, why didn't you get a search warrant today?"

"I wanted to try talking to him first. He's retirement age. I expected him to be home."

Fiona followed the Impala to a big stone church. "She was telling the truth about the funeral anyway," Fiona said.

Lollie parked and walked gingerly in her high-heeled boots toward a side door of the church. As they drove by, they saw Lollie slip on the icy surface and almost go down.

"Whoa," Eddie said. "Lollie and her tater-tot hotdish almost bit the dust, but I'm so hungry I'd eat it off the blacktop."

"That hungry, huh?"

"Yeah. Know anyplace that serves tater-tot hotdish?"

"Really?" Fiona said as she raised a brow. She drove to Jersey Mike's for sandwiches.

As they ate, Fiona and Eddie discussed the case.

"Maybe the Filstrom's son killed Vonn," Navarre offered, "because he found out about his mother and Vonn."

"Assuming there was an affair, but I'm pleased you're considering other scenarios."

"Trying to be objective."

"Thomas was fourteen at the time, so he's twenty-four now. I'm going to drop by his place tonight. Maybe Arnold is there. Also, the Rose family is coming in later this afternoon. They lived across the street from the Purcells at the time and Thomas had slept at their house the night Vonn was murdered. They also moved off Garfield after the murder."

Fiona drove to the MPD building on Fifth Street. While she did paperwork on Lollie's interview, she thought about Lollie's demeanor. For someone who knew nothing about the murder, she sure was nervous.

At five o'clock, Mr. and Mrs. Rose and their son, Paul, arrived, all wearing dark suits. The family owned and operated Rose Funeral Home in Minneapolis. They were pleasant and cooperative, but none had any new information about Vonn's murder or Arnold Purcell's whereabouts. Paul said he was still friends with Thomas, but his parents said they didn't maintain contact with Lollie and Arnold Purcell.

Early evening, Fiona took the Hennepin Avenue Bridge to University Avenue. Thomas Purcell lived in an apartment smelling of pizza on Fifth Avenue SE. He was a Chris Farley look-alike in a Metro Transit uniform, and he didn't appear surprised to see her. Lollie must have warned him.

"Thomas, we're relooking at the open-unsolved homicide of your former neighbor."

"Mr. Vonn. That was a long time ago."

"Ten years. I understand you were across the street at Paul Rose's house that night. Now that you're older, you may recall something that could help us."

"All I remember was the storm and the power going out and we had to play cards with flashlights instead of playing Paul's new video games. The next morning, we saw cop cars at Vonn's house."

"We need to talk to your dad, Thomas. Is he here?"

He shook his head.

Fiona waited him out for more information.

"Mom said he was up north," he said. Blotches appeared on his cheeks.

"Your mother's driving their only vehicle. Does he have access to another?"

The blotches widened. "I wouldn't know."

"When was the last time you spoke to your dad?"

He grimaced. "Not in a while. We never did get along."

"I'm sorry to hear that," Fiona said. He answered further questions but gave her nothing new.

Fiona and Eddie took turns surveilling the Purcell residence for ten days. No Arnold coming or going. To keep up the pressure, they checked in with Lollie Purcell daily either by phone or a knock at the door.

Considering Arnold Purcell's apparent absence, Fiona secured a search warrant. Eddie and Fiona knocked on Purcell's door at 7:30 a.m. on a Monday morning, with a crew standing by.

It took Lollie a few minutes to answer the door. Dressed in a pink fleece bathrobe and matching slippers, and without excessive make-up, she looked different, normal, until she grabbed the warrant and screamed at them, "I told you he's not home! But go ahead. Search for yourself!"

Fiona and her team checked the entire two-story residence, including the basement, garage, and gardening shed. No Arnold, but she did gather clues. Fiona pulled the team together in the four-season porch off the dining room.

She said, "I find it strange the men's clothing in the closet is dusty, and there's only women's clothing in the laundry hamper. We need to get the son over here."

An hour later, a patrol unit showed up with Thomas wearing his Metro Transit uniform.

"Did we pull you off your route?" Fiona asked.

He nodded, asking, "What's the emergency?"

"There are indications your father doesn't live here anymore."

He let out a sigh as his concerned expression morphed to resignation.

"Follow me," he said.

Fiona and Eddie followed Thomas to the kitchen. Lollie moved after him like a feral cat, snarling and hissing. "Damn it, Tommy."

He shook his head. "I can't do this anymore, Mom."

He took the snowman cookie jar off the counter and placed it on the kitchen table. He lifted the lid and pulled out a bag of cookies. Perplexed, Fiona looked inside.

"I take it these are your husband's ashes in the cookie jar, Mrs. Purcell. I'm confused why his death wasn't reported," Fiona said.

Lollie gestured her head toward her son. "Ask Tommy."

"Tommy?" Fiona asked.

"He died in his sleep. We found him dead still in his chair with the television on. Mom begged me not to call 911. She said if Dad's company knew he died, they'd cut off his pension. She couldn't support us without it."

Fiona shook her head in disbelief. A new one on her.

"When?" she asked.

"Two thousand eleven," Thomas said.

"You would have been what? Sixteen?"

Thomas nodded.

"But he's cremated. Were the Roses complicit in the coverup by not recording his death?"

Thomas shook his head. "No way. Paul's folks didn't know. Still don't. They were away on vacation and Paul was staying with us. He'd already been training with his dad and knew how to operate the crematorium, so we decided it was our only option."

Fiona wasn't sure Arnold wasn't poisoned, or bludgeon like Vonn. "Thomas, did your father really die of natural causes?"

"Yes, I'm the one who found him," he said. "Mom was real upset."

Fiona took a deep breath. "So, who killed Frederick Vonn?"

Looking mighty sorrowful, Lollie said, "Arnold."

Thomas shook his head. "No, Mom, you did."

Lollie swiveled her head toward her son. "How would you know?"

"I overheard you and Dad arguing. You said you and Mr. Vonn were in love, and he wanted you to move to Florida with him, but Dad said you were delusional, that Mr. Vonn rejected you. You got angry at Vonn and hit him with the spade. Dad cleaned up your mess."

Lollie appeared stunned.

"But Detective Carlson verified you were at your mother's that night," Fiona said.

As her words flowed, Lollie stared at the cookie jar. "When I told Arnold what happened, he told me to go to my mother's, to take my bloody clothes, and a few of Fred's things to make it look like a robbery, and throw them in a dumpster along the way."

"Arnold covered for you."

"Yes, but I paid the price," Lollie said, her face stretched with angst. "He dropped his life insurance policy and made sure I didn't get his pension checks when he died. He said I could take care of myself, but I couldn't live on social security alone."

"Didn't Arnold feel a responsibility to provide for Thomas?" Fiona asked.

Lollie began sobbing.

Thomas shook his head. "Dad was too angry and vindictive to think clearly. He was mentally ill. May I speak to you privately, Detective?" he asked Fiona.

He led her back into the porch. "I'm sorry I wasn't truthful earlier."

"That would have been nice."

"I can't keep this secret anymore. I always felt I had to protect Mom. She's not right either. She talks to him, takes his ashes for rides. That's not healthy, is it?"

"I don't know. I'm not a psychiatrist," Fiona said.

"Are Paul and I in trouble?"

"The county attorney will decide, but this is an unusual case."

Fiona returned to the kitchen and arrested Lollie for the murder of Frederick Vonn and the failure to report the death of Arnold Purcell.

DNA analysis of bone fragments from the ashes proved to be Arnold Purcell's. Although Thomas and Paul Rose played a role in the coverup by cremating Arnold's remains, they were not charged. The county prosecutor held Mrs. Purcell culpable, and because she never reported Arnold's death to Social Security, the Feds also charged her with defrauding the government.

Midge Bubany is the author of four published police-procedural mystery novels set in north central Minnesota and four short stories in anthologies. Midge has studied writing at the Loft Literary Center and has educated herself on police procedures using several resources, including attending the Orono Citizens Police Academy and the Hennepin County Sheriff's Law Enforcement Citizens Academy. She is a member of Women of Words and the Twin Cities Sisters in Crime. Midge lives with her dog, Juni, in the western suburbs of Minneapolis.

The Long Goodbye
ANN AUBITZ

— ❧ —

As I ran through the tall yellow sunflowers, the morning sun shone brightly through the giant flowers in the fields and warmed my face. I ran back toward the farmhouse and smelled smoke. It burned my lungs, and at once, the bile swirled in my stomach as dread and helplessness washed over me. Next, I heard the piercing screams of my parents, and their voices rang in my ears. I knew something was wrong, and I needed to get to them. I knew it, but my feet would not move. I was paralyzed amid the sunflowers, unable to help my parents as flames engulfed our farmhouse. Then, I heard the buzz of the military drones flying overhead in the smoky sky. I dropped to the ground and buried myself deep in the damp soil and leaves to camouflage my body. I stayed hidden for hours and then slowly walked toward the farmhouse. My petite body quivered as I stared at the horrific sight. Our lovely home was a smoldering pile of *black ash. I screamed out for my mom and dad, but it was futile. They were gone.*

I felt something hit my head. Then, I realized it was my roommate's pillow.

"Sorry, was I dreaming again?" I wiped my tears on my sleeve.

"More like screaming again. You need help, like serious help," screamed Dara. Her face scrunched up and red as she yelled at me.

"I'm sorry, I had the dream about my family again."

"Cry me a river, Willow. We all know the story of how your perfect life ended when you were five years old, and you were ripped from your Minnesota farm and brought to this hellhole by your horrible grandmother."

"Oh, shut up, Dara," came another voice. "You know Willow saw her parents die, and she still feels responsible for their death."

I winced when Tina said this, knowing she was only trying to stick up for me, but she said it so abruptly that it was almost cruel.

Nevertheless, Tina was most like me, born on Earth and brought to the Planetary Government Boarding School for Girls. Tina hated tension and confrontation, which was pretty much constant in our dorm room these days.

Dara got out of her bed and stood in front of Tina. "I can't wait to graduate this month and get away from you, Tina. I am so tired of you sticking up for Willow. She needs to learn what it is like out there. It's not all flowers and sunshine."

"I know the world is not all flowers and sunshine, Dara," I muttered, hoping she didn't hear me so she wouldn't lash out again. As I looked at Dara I thought: *I see vicious green vines wrapping around her neck, squeezing the life out of her until there is no breath left in her limp body. Then, finally, the vines drop her to the ground with a sickening thud. As the rest of us watch in absolute silence, I find it hard to be remorseful, as it is finally my moment of vindication against Dara for all the pain she has caused me.* I shake my head and see Dara standing in the same place as she was before, still battling with Tina. I suspect I am slowly and unequivocally losing my mind.

Although Dara thinks of me as child-like, I fully understand our world's current state, and it is not idyllic. Earth is the controlling planet in the ruling body called the Planetary Government. We have a new Supreme Chancellor whose judgment is steadfast that humans are superior in every way to other beings of alien or non-alien origin. Therefore, he believes humans should politically and economically govern non-humanoid people. I remember when the ruling government of Earth welcomed people from all the planets. I wish it were still like this.

I better stop daydreaming of the perfect life and get a move on. Unfortunately, I have a meeting first thing this morning with the very dreadful Headmistress Yvonne, who has been in charge of our school on the space station for a little over a year. When Headmistress Yvonne arrived, all our privileges were immediately revoked, like the freedom to roam the space station, meet new people, and hang out in the common areas. It was about the same time my roommates and I started fighting.

When I look at the Headmistress, I see tree branches and vines coming through the wall behind her head.

There is surprise and agony on her face as the branches wrap around her arms and legs, threatening to separate them from her torso. The thick green vines pull her limbs in opposite directions. I can hear the sounds of her ripping cartilage...

"Willow, are you paying attention?"

I put my head in my hands to block out the images. I have to figure out what is happening to me. These horrible images are occurring more often and becoming more violent every day.

She repeated the question, louder this time. "Willow Marie Martin, are you paying attention? You need to decide what you will do when you leave here next month." Headmistress gave me an impatient look and tapped her two-inch blue nails on her new mahogany desk. "You are the only graduating senior who has not chosen a job with the Planetary Government. You should be thankful you have this option."

"I don't want any of those jobs. All those jobs are in the cities or on the space stations. I want to live in a vast open space again and feel the sun on my face."

Oh, how I missed the sun on my face. Truthfully even the nightmares are welcome because they are the only time I can see my favorite place in the whole world: Minnesota. Some people may prefer to live in the big cities, with the large buildings and millions of people, but not me. I fondly remember spending my days in the fields with my dad and the nights roasting marshmallows with my mom. Suddenly I remembered where I was and tuned in to hear what Headmistress Yvonne said.

"Willow, you know these are the only jobs available to girls without families. They are good steady jobs, much better than you deserve."

"No offense, Headmistress Yvonne, but I know I can do more than work in a kitchen or a factory. I believe I can do more than those menial jobs. I can feel it."

Headmistress Yvonne shoved the paper in my face and snorted. "You cannot do more than this, nor do you deserve more. You are lucky to get anything. These are the positions that are open to you. Pick one NOW!"

I ran from the office and headed to my private sanctuary—the arboretum. The plants are my friends. When I am lonely, they comfort me. When I am sad, they make me happy. They also remind me of my parents and the farm, especially the sunflowers. It is the only connection to Minnesota I have left.

I heard the door open and saw my botany teacher strolling in. Dr. Carol Carver looked around at the flowers, then tossed a quizzical look at me. All of the flowers around me are closed or are in a wilted state. She has often mentioned how the plants seem to take on my mood when I visit them. If I am happy, they are in full bloom. When I am miserable, they are wilted and sad too.

"What's up, buttercup?"

"Funny, Dr. Carver. What makes you think something is wrong?" I said sarcastically, looking around at the wilted flowers.

"Well, I know you had a meeting with Headmistress Yvonne, and I can guess by your mood, the meeting didn't go as well as you hoped."

"It didn't. The headmistress wouldn't even listen to me. She told me the only jobs available for girls without families are on the list. She wants me to pick a menial job with the Planetary Government and leave her space station. I don't have a choice. I will have to pick one, so I can go."

"Willow, what if I told you there is another choice?" She whispered this last statement and looked around the room. We were the only two in the arboretum, yet she sat for a moment without saying a word. "I have a plan."

Feeling dizzy as I often do as I walked through the long, dreary corridor back to my dorm room, I thought about the cryptic conversation I had in the arboretum with Dr. Carver, who left before telling me her "plan." She had simply stood up and left the room. I called after her, but she ignored me. That's Dr. Carver for you. She is an odd duck, but she has been like a mother to me.

When I reached the door of my room I heard the sound of breaking glass coming from inside. Dara was at it again, screaming at the top of her lungs at Tina. My hand trembled as I reached for the doorknob. I bit my lip and tightened my fingers around the cold knob. I was stalling, not wanting to go in but knowing I had to save Tina from Dara's wrath. After all, Tina did stick up for me yesterday.

"Hello ladies, how are things going?"

"Oh, shut up, Willow. I am not in the mood for your crap." Dara violently stomped around the room and bolted past me into the hallway, slamming the door so hard I felt the vibrations through the soles of my shoes.

"Good riddance," Tina mumbled under her breath.

"Why is she so upset? I haven't seen her this mad since she failed her history final."

"She didn't get the job she wanted, so she decided to take it out on your poor plant and me," Tina pointed to the shattered pot and mangled plant on the floor.

"Oh, poor thing." I picked up the plant and gently set it in a mug. Once I touched it, the plant sprang back to life, and the bloom became bigger than ever. Tina at first pretended not to notice the flower looked better now than before it had been smashed, but eventually spoke up.

"You are so good with plants. How do you do that?"

"I'm not sure. Plants just respond to me."

Dara returned about an hour later, still in a rotten mood. I pretended to be asleep on my cot. Unfortunately, my trick didn't work, and she pulled a strand of my spiky blonde hair and screamed in my face, "Headmistress Yvonne wants to see you now. Have fun!"

I headed out the door and down the same long, drab corridor. Finally, I reached Headmistress Yvonne's office, took a deep breath, and walked in. She sat behind her desk with a smug look on her overly made-up face. "You will be transported to another facility effective immediately." She handed me a sheet, pretended to study the papers on her desk, and added, "Your transport leaves in the morning. That will be all."

"What facility? I still have time to pick a job, and graduation isn't for another month." I held onto the wall to steady myself. This place is hell most of the time—but it had been my home for thirteen years.

"You will not be graduating. Instead, you will move to a clinical study facility on Earth. Your orders came in today. Pack your stuff. You will be leaving for the first transport tomorrow morning." Her impatience with me grew with every word she spat out of her unpleasant mouth. She tried dismissing me again— but I wouldn't leave.

The branches and vines come out of the ceiling, wrapping around her skinny neck with alarming swiftness, lifting her out of her chair and dangling her by her neck. Her feet are kicking in the air, trying to gain traction, and reaching the floor to no avail. The vines are strangling her, and all I hear is a faint gurgling noise, then silence.

I shook my head to rid myself of the horrendous image so that I could continue my argument with the headmistress. A thought crossed my mind that I should tell someone about the imagery I have seen lately, but at that moment, it was not my primary concern.

"Headmistress Yvonne, please tell me why I won't be graduating and will be leaving so soon. Please, you owe me that much." My voice came out as a whisper, "Please."

"Willow, I don't owe you anything. You have been the bane of my existence since I arrived at this school, and I am glad to see you go. Do you know how many times your roommates tried to have you removed from their quarters? A lot. Now, get out of my office. You will be given further instructions tomorrow morning." She was so mad at me that her voice came out as a high-pitched shriek.

I finally gathered my wits and left Headmistress Yvonne's office without another glance from her. She doesn't care about me, about any of us. It's only a job for her.

I knew it was late, but I needed to see Dr. Carver to say goodbye and to thank her for her support and friendship for all these years. She wasn't in her quarters, so I looked in the next logical place, the arboretum. When I walked in, she didn't look surprised to see me. Instead, it seemed as if she was expecting me. I stood in the doorway for a moment and started to sob. She came over immediately and dried my tears with her scarf. "Honey, don't cry. You will be okay. It is all part of my master plan. You will be out of here and away from nasty Headmistress Yvonne. You are right. You do not belong in one of the awful Planetary Government positions. You are so special, more than you even know."

"What do you mean special? Headmistress Yvonne said I am the bane of her existence."

"Don't listen to that old bat. You are incredible. You have powers you haven't yet discovered. But you know it deep down inside, so release them, and I promise good things will happen to you."

"I will miss you so much."

"Willow, I know you will see me again. I guarantee it," she said while hugging me hard. "Now, I want you to do something for me. Come over here and make these flowers bloom. They are all wilted."

I walked over to the bright pink Gerber Daisies and waved my hand over the top of them. They all opened as if by magic.

I said my final goodbyes to Dr. Carver and walked back to my dorm room. I am sure my roommates will be devastated I am leaving. Not.

I got to my room, and my roommates were asleep. It was after midnight, and I knew I was leaving first thing in the morning, so I needed to sleep too, but I kept thinking about what new facility I would be moving to tomorrow. I would never sleep in this bed again, hear Dara yell at Tina, or visit the arboretum. I finally dozed off.

My mom is humming as she pulls my long strands of blonde hair through her tiny fingers. It's a song she used to sing to me every night. Then, finally, she stops brushing my hair, looks directly into my eyes, and says, "You have special powers, my darling, and you must use them for good."

I woke up wishing I had another minute with my mom. I realized my roommates were already up and dressed.

"Well, nice of you to wake up sleeping beauty. You better get a move on. You don't want to miss your transport. I would say I will miss you, but I won't," Dara snarled.

"What do you mean? Are you leaving, Willow? Before graduation?" Tina acted genuinely sad to see me go. Then I remember Tina will be on her own with Dara.

"I am going to miss you, Willow." Tina hugged me. "Good luck. I know you will be great."

What a strange thing to say to me. Frankly, I was a little paranoid. I felt like everyone knew where I was going except for me. So what did Tina mean? I know you will be great? Great at what?

I said goodbye to all the girls in the dorm, and Tina hugged me again. Saundra grunted, and Dara snarled. That's okay. I am out of here. I started getting excited about leaving. I packed up the few things I owned, threw my bag over my shoulder, and headed to the arboretum.

I walked through the main door as I expected Dr. Carver to be waiting for me on my favorite bench. Saying our last goodbyes are the hardest thing I have ever had to do. She assured me she will see me again, but I wish I knew that. She offered to take me the transport, but I decide I don't need a longer goodbye.

And now, looking back on today, I traveled on a transport, a plane, a bus, a train, and finally, I made it to the research facility, and it was literally out in the middle of nowhere. I was exhausted and anxious. My butt was sore, my legs were numb, and to make things worse, the guy seated next to me fell asleep and drooled all over my shoulder. But, even with the drool, I knew that I was in a much better place for me. Finally, I arrived at my new home with the beautiful sun shining on my face.

What a shock! I looked out the window, and there is Dr. Carver. Well, I guess we really didn't need the long goodbye.

Ann Aubitz is the Co-owner and Publisher of Kirk House Publishers and FuzionPress, located in Burnsville, Minnesota. After years of reading everything she could get her hands on, she decided to help others achieve their dream of becoming an author. Her mission is to help authors reach their objectives by seeing their books in print.

Ann is also a proud member of the Independent Book Publishers Association, a Board Member-At-Large for the Midwest Independent Publishers Association, and a group leader for Women of Words and chairs the yearly WOW writing conference.

Kirkhousepublishers.com

STORY 16

Of Love and Loss

MARY KAY CRAWFORD

At the Minnesota Twins Opener, in the open-air ballpark, I watch you crack and drop roasted peanut shells onto the concrete slab flooring. With eyes riveted on the oversized scoreboard, you greedily consume a half bag of nuts with the same intensity whales use to devour up to 20 tons of seafood each day.

A messy smattering of discarded peanut shells lay strewn at your feet. Their dusty shell carcasses like so many girlfriends you found fault with. Grew tired of. Through no fault of your own, you've mentioned.

You turn to me with judgment in your eyes and ask, "Do you even understand baseball? The rules of scorekeeping?"

"I'm not a scorekeeper," I say, drawing back. "I watch the athleticism, the gestures and posture of the players. How they prance with high knees, across the field during warm-ups. How their agile bodies turn to swing at the bat with crackerjack speed. It's impressive," I say, sensing your disapproval of my carnal enjoyment of the game.

Last month, for one week, we vacationed at your Florida condo. A condo, decorated years earlier by your first wife, Sue.

"Why did you leave your first wife?" I ask.

"She left her underwear in the middle of the floor," you answer with garlic breath.

Sue had chosen wallpaper splashed with jumbo palm fronds in tropical shades of lime and aqua, a square rattan coffee table and complimentary floral rattan sofa, a palm leaf patterned bedspread with sunshine-themed throw pillows, an asparagus-colored refrigerator and flamingo-pink shuttered closet doors. An atmosphere reminiscent of the *Golden Girls* TV sitcom. *A wonderfully immersive experience*, I thought with a subtle eye roll.

And there were trinkets strewn throughout the condo. On end-tables and heightened kitchen counter tops. Stir sticks and coasters from the Holland ship cruise line. Voyages you enjoyed with Kelly, and Vicky, and Renee.

Ship's photos, still displayed long after the break-up with each woman, individually framed in similar poses. You had a story for each, or at least the ones you remembered.

But it was Jayne spelled with a "y" that I thought of now and what to do if ever I saw her. "She'll be sitting in the hallway, on the floor, by my condo door reading a book, looking morose," you say. "That's Jayne. Just turn and walk the other way as though you don't know me or that I live here."

It had been an "ugly break-up," you told me. Her yelling, "You don't understand! You don't understand!" before screeching away from your downtown brick residence in her car.

Next day, a mysterious case of vodka arriving at your condo, without a note. But you knew it was from Jayne. She hoped you would guzzle the potent alcohol, stumble, fall and crack your head on the coffee table. Then die.

When you were still a couple, there was that threatening note Jayne left one evening before heading out. She had removed all the kitchen knives from your drawers and arranged them in a circular fashion like so many drawn swords, pointy ends facing a picture she had quickly sketched. A part of your anatomy you were especially fond of. It was meant as a warning. Be fiercely loyal or…be dismembered. "Not *disremembered*", you clarified for my benefit, "but *dismembered.*"

Another girlfriend—not Jayne—became so enraged she slammed your sliding patio screen door with such violence it fell off its track.

"I was fond of her," you said, shaking your head sadly.

That's when you were the pilot, the captain working for a prestigious airline, and she was the flight attendant ready to stir your drink.

Ultimately, however, it was the vodka you were most enthusiastic about.

"A good pour," was the phrase you used often, as a way to compliment the bartender and to encourage a heavy-handed pour of that freezer chilled Polish vodka. Addictive and intoxicating.

"Why me?" I wondered. I had shiny auburn hair that swept down my back and an inviting smile. Fourteen years younger than you. I wasn't violent or vengeful. I had a job with great benefits. Free concert tickets. Free theater tickets. Free TWINS tickets.

Another girlfriend would have grown tired of your querulous voice and admonishments—and moved on.

Another girlfriend would have sensed your lack of interest in her—*and interest only in yourself.*

Another girlfriend would have left the stadium abruptly. Would have turned to look back and observed you seated alone with a dazed and gaping expression, your bag of peanuts still in hand.

But the first-base seat tickets were mine. Seats with extensive views of the Minneapolis skyline. My employer had offered the tickets to me, and I accepted. Just as I had accepted so much else that didn't belong to me. *I was never meant to have.*

This early spring day there is a chill in the air. The sky is an overcast gloomy gray as I bundle myself warmly into my stadium jacket, zipping it closed to cover this frayed and seasoned heart that knows well the rush of love and loss.

First, I blame the weather for the disappointment I feel on this day.

Then, I blame myself for the slow awakening of my relinquished heart.

Why do I not believe what I already know of love and loss—and you?

No more amazement, I say. Game over, I say.

It is the sort of day to be alone in.

Then rather like a dream, I pass through the stadium on a cloudscape of solitude, pressing into the spring wind, and do not look back.

 Mary K Crawford-Lorfink has been published in *WINK: Writers in the Know* magazine, *Creatopia* magazine and Amazon books, graduated with a BA in English from the U of MN, is an ongoing student at The Loft Literary Center, Minneapolis, MN, and a member of WOW - Women of Words. 'Writing is a mystical experience – turning wonder into story'

Lucky that Way

JANICE STROOTMAN

She sat perched atop the dented overturned milk pail at the entrance to the barn and rubbed her grimy hands on her faded dungarees. The warm spring sunshine shone on her sensitive skin as she took in the waking sounds of the animals rustling around in the hay-strewn pens behind her and the chirping birds as they clung tightly to the telephone wires overhead. The pungent smell of fresh straw underfoot tickled her nose and caused her to sneeze. "Isn't it interesting how my life turned out?" she mused as she watched Nola, her favorite Guernsey milk cow slowly chewing her cud across the barnyard from her. "All I wanted was to be famous," she said aloud as she met Nola's chocolate brown eyes gazing steadily at her.

Now, here she was, back where she started, on her parents' farm in a small rural town in southern Minnesota, trying to avoid the spotlight she once had wanted so much. Her quest for fame hadn't come to fruition, at least not in the way she had imagined. She was so hell-bent on getting out of town after high school that she hadn't laid down a solid plan for accomplishing her dream. Of course, what did she really know at the tender age of seventeen, and fresh out of high school?

Her parents had provided her with a carefree childhood full of tree climbing, caring for the animals, playing "kick the can" with the neighboring farm children, and swimming in the creek during the sticky, sweaty days of summer. They tried to understand her restlessness and kept her busy with chores of slopping the pigs, mucking out the barn, and feeding the chickens, but the restlessness persisted. They had hoped she would attend the local college only twelve miles away that offered numerous nationally ranked undergraduate programs, but she wasn't interested.

She didn't lack attention in high school. Her Scandinavian roots had blessed her with an enviable peaches-and-cream complexion, sparkling blue eyes, natural strawberry blonde hair, and striking features. A high metabolism rate and farm chores kept her body toned and sculpted. "I'm lucky that way," she thought.

She found the boys in her class to be dorky and short-sighted, not interested in adventures outside of their rural community. The girls seemed mostly jealous of her beauty. Looking back, she realized she had kept herself back, staying aloof from others because she felt destined for greater things.

When she left for Los Angeles on a tired, dusty greyhound bus the day after graduation, she didn't look back. The expressions on her parents' faces at the breakfast table the morning she left would haunt her forever. They sat, shoulders hunched, eyes downcast, sad and silent as they glanced at her, looks of dismay and agony on their faces.

As the miles flashed by, she watched in anticipation for signs that the "big city" of L.A. was approaching. Resting her head on the window glass, she smiled to herself as she imagined the huge, ornate mansions she would see and the talent scouts that would be scanning the streets looking for fresh new stars—like her!

As she sat immersed in her fantasies, the continuous drone of the bus wheels lulled her to sleep. She was jolted awake by the sound of screaming brakes, people yelling, and the feeling of being tossed around, tumbling over and over again like wet, limp laundry in a clothes dryer. When the rolling stopped, everything seemed to move in slow motion. Was she hurt? Could she move? The silence surrounding her was all encompassing. She slowly became aware of the nauseating smell of gasoline. "I have to get out of here!" she shrieked. No sooner had the words left her mouth than she heard a loud "poof" and the crinkling of glass breaking. The bus was on fire!

Her mind seemed to crawl along as slowly as her body as she tried to dislodge herself from several backpacks, part of an upholstered bus seat, and two hard-sided suitcases. She felt a surge of heat and realized she was crawling toward the blast rather than away from it. Her mind was screaming "help" but her voice was silent. *I'm going to die! Everyone is going to die!* she feared. Just as she struggled to turn back, another explosion hit her full-on. It felt like her face was melting. Her nerves screamed in agony as she sank into unconsciousness.

The next thing she remembered was the sound of high-pitched "beeps" of lifesaving monitors, and the blurry glare of florescent light piercing through the slit in her eye bandages as she lay motionless on the steel-framed hospital bed.

As she was the only survivor of the crash, she was inundated with questions from reporters around the country who wanted to know about the accident and why she was going to Los Angeles on her own. It took months of painful recovery and grueling rehabilitation to enable her to return home to the farm. Yes, indeed! She had wanted to be famous and now she was, though not in the way she had fantasized.

The sound of Nora's bellow and the clanging of her cowbell brought her out of her reverie. Even though she was well known around town and had been born and raised there, she was now referred to by the locals as the "burned girl." Her parents and the farm animals were the only ones that didn't flinch when they looked at her.

She shook her head and gingerly touched her face. "I'm lucky that way," she sighed.

 Jan is a retired kindergarten teacher who in October 2022 published her first book, *Child Heart, Notes from a Kindergarten Teacher,* a compilation of stories about teaching in Minnesota, Hong Kong, Belarus, and Slovakia. Her work has been published in MinnPost, Cathay Pacific magazine, and WINK magazine. She lives in Bloomington with her husband Denny and little dog, Ellie. She enjoys her writing groups that include WOW (Women of Words), PINK (Poets in the Know), National League of American Pen Women, and taking classes at the LOFT Literary Center in Minneapolis.

The Medicine Woman
NADIA GIORDANA

T he old woman walked alone on this cool, Minnesota morning, with only a blanket, a bearskin, a small ration of food, her medicine bag, and a tightly woven basket. She continued until she found an area by a stream that she felt was the perfect place. It was already dusk when she arrived, so she rolled up in her fur and slept until morning.

When it was light, she quickly cleared a place and began to build a sweat lodge. Its construction took her all day. She used branches and pine boughs and leaves to make a rather small dome-shaped enclosure with a pit in the middle of the floor and an opening at the side to be used as a door. Over the door, she hung her blanket.

During all this time, and even the day before, she had eaten nothing save for a tea made from the bark of a tree.

When her holy place was ready, she built a large fire over a bed of rocks just outside the lodge. The fire burned all night, and all night she sat there and tended it, singing her ritual songs and chants and praying for her "Dream Person" to bring her a vision soon.

At dawn, she placed a mound of the glowing rocks into the pit inside the crude sweat lodge. Then she removed her clothes, and with her basket filled with water, and a small pot to be used as a ladle, she entered the lodge to purify herself.

Once inside, she sat down in the cross-legged position on her bearskin and began to splash water onto hot rocks. She began to sing, chant and pray. She continued this ceremony for several hours, adding more rocks as needed, until her body could no longer endure the heat and the steam.

Dripping with sweat, she left the lodge and walked over to the stream and plunged into the cold water, immersing herself completely in the refreshing coolness of it.

After she had finished and gotten dressed, she brewed herself a different tea made of dried wild mushrooms and herbs that she kept in her medicine bag. It was mildly euphoric.

Darkness was coming again so she took her blanket and went to the spot where she would now spend the third night. It wasn't far from her sweat lodge. When she got there, she took from her bag a small offering of tobacco and gently sprinkled it on the ground, whispering a soft prayer as she prepared the sacred place. Next, she found four stones. The first one was reddish, the second was white, another was black, and the last one was yellow. These were to signify the four winds. The red was for the south, and she placed it in the south end of her sacred circle. The black stone she placed in the west, and the white stone she put at the north end of the circle. Finally, she placed the yellow stone at the east side of the circle. Then she made another prayer, entered the circle from the east, laid down her blanket, and sat down and crossed her legs.

She was old and had done this many times before whenever she had needed assistance from the dream world. Once it became fully dark, she again began to sing songs and to pray. This time each song or prayer was repeated four times before she began the next one. It was close to midnight when she had finished, and she just sat there and patiently waited.

There was a crescent moon that gave the entire area just enough light to cast faint shadows on the ground and to make the outline of the trees clearly visible against the night sky. The wind came in random gusts that swirled playfully around her, and then died down to a faint rustle before it sprang up again. Then as she stared into the darkness, she saw him—the Great Yellow Bear, her most powerful totem animal.

As he began to speak to her, she stood up and watched and listened intently until he finished. She then nodded in understanding, closed her eyes, and gave a prayer of thanks. When she opened her eyes, he was gone as she knew he would be. She had her answers now, so she gathered up her blanket and went back to the sweat lodge. It was almost morning of the fourth day, and she was hungry.

She built another fire and made herself a stew of dried meat and grains using the same small pot she had used as a ladle. After she had eaten, she dismantled the lodge and scattered the branches about, picked up her things, and began the long walk back to the village.

Nadia Gíordana is a producer and community TV host in the Minneapolis/Saint Paul metro area. She strives to shine a spotlight on talented and deserving women. One of the best ways she does this is via multiple interview series she produces. She is also the publisher and executive editor of WINK: Writers IN the Know literary magazine. It offers a platform for writers to see their work published in an international venue.

Mom's Lessons Never End

TAMMY LAURENT

W ith the concrete hot under my feet, I pushed the wheelchair along the bumpy sidewalks of the small town in western Minnesota. It had been named Canby, after General Edward Canby, an assassinated Army man in the Civil War. The petunias were starting to wilt in the heat. The dogs, after digging a hole, sprawled lazily in the dirt, trying to soak up the coolness of the earth.

We walked and walked, some days ten miles or more. It seemed like the easiest thing to do. Conversation was hard, her wheelchair making a thump, thump, thump as we crossed the cracks in the sidewalks—sidewalks that had been there my whole life. Some of them were rusted from well water used to water the grass. Some of them were newly cracked from the harsh winter a few months before. Because of the thumping, it was preferable to walk, run, bike or wheel right down the middle of the street, which was not an unusual sight.

"Let's go over there." She would point in a nondescript way, but I knew what she meant. Mom loved nothing more than a trip to the Dairy Queen, especially on a hot, windless day such as this. It was definitely time for a strawberry sundae. She used to love chocolate with pecans, but her lack of teeth made that impossible these days.

Before the stroke, we talked endlessly of life and trips, family and struggles. Now conversation was limited to whatever I could think of that would interest her or encourage some kind of participation with her limited vocabulary.

As we marched along, me, the pusher, and Mom enjoying the ride, I always felt amazed at the cars that slow, even a half block early, to let us go past. They often wave and yell out a greeting. It's the town I grew up in. Everyone knew we were headed to the Dairy Queen, because, like most small towns, everyone knew everything.

Later that evening, I would run into many of them who would ask how my mom was doing and comment on how far we must have walked. They had driven past us several times. Sympathy showed in their eyes. They knew it wasn't easy.

Mom had always been a significant part of life in Canby. She taught Sunday School, went to all the wrestling matches, even after my brothers had long graduated, ran the Junior Auxiliary, headed up numerous committees, and volunteered for more jobs than anyone could count. All the people who knew her shook their heads in agreement that this wasn't fair for a woman so full of life.

They knew of her stroke, the damned wheelchair, and of the patience we had when she'd say, "I thought you'd forgotten about me. You never come to see me anymore."

In truth, we came to see her all the time, but her memory was getting short. And her time in the nursing home was getting long.

I wouldn't choose anywhere else to grow up. We didn't have all the luxuries of life, but we always had food on the table, a roof over our head, and a loving family around us. We didn't know there were things we didn't have because no one else had them either.

Our youth was spent getting wet and dirty, splashing around in the creek, playing in the barn loft, and adding on to our substantial tree house. Our toys were never purchased. They were large sticks for swords, rocks for building materials, and an old chicken coop, where the nesting boxes made great kitchen cabinets for delicious mud pies.

Mom loved her gardens, her black lab, Whiley, with a head bigger than a state-fair pumpkin, and her friends, who she met with on a regular basis. They called themselves the "Just Us Club," for lack of a better name.

Mom and Dad had been together for most of their lives. They began as high school sweethearts and lasted through a separation as Dad enlisted in the Navy for WWII. When he returned, he thought it would be fun to surprise her by sneaking up on her in the local theatre. Many years later, with five kids, and six grandkids, they celebrated their 50th wedding anniversary.

Of the five kids in my family, two of us looked the part of blonde Minnesota Norwegians, while the other three had brown hair, brown eyes, and looked more like my mother's Danish roots.

We thought Mom would live forever, unlike my father. Dad's last day was like many he had. He woke up early and had coffee in the small-town restaurant/bar with his buddies. They always met early because if you were still farming, it was a great way to get news and a little camaraderie before you headed out to the field. If you were retired, like Dad, you still woke up that early by habit, so you might as well go in for coffee and enjoy the banter. In the afternoon, he went fishing for northern pike in one of the 10,000 lakes. We never knew if he caught anything, because most of the guys released their fish back into the wild. I didn't know if it was because he didn't want to clean them, or if Mom already had plans for supper.

Late in the day, Dad returned home for a nap in the green chair. After supper, he went to bed and, on that fateful day, never woke up. As shocking as it was to all of us, we realize now what a gift he was given—the gift of a fast ending and not having to live without your life partner. Mom wouldn't be so lucky.

Well into her 80's, Mom loved to be in her garden pulling weeds, watering flowers and picking vegetables. Her hands were strong, her skin rough from hoeing or digging, her nails uneven from hard manual labor. She never imagined she would lose the ability to work with her hands, particularly her right one. It would become soft, shriveled, useless, with clean nails all the same length.

She has those hearty Scandinavian roots so many Minnesota women have. Genes that made us believe she would live to 102 and still be living on the farm. Our confidence fell the day we learned of her brain bleed. So unfair that a woman with that much vitality could be brought down by something so small. So powerful.

The brain bleed, which we've decided to call a stroke, was definitely a life-changing event. Living on a low-maintenance farm road isn't for the weak of heart. Mom paid someone to clear snow from the driveway and to clear out the two miles of gravel road to the highway. Often it wasn't cleared for days after a storm, leaving her stranded in the century-old farmhouse where her family had lived for over 120 years. During big blizzards and electrical outages, she would hunker down, spend time by candlelight, but never leave Wiley and the twenty cats unfed in the barn.

This was the lifestyle we were used to. It was common for us to wait days for a return phone call. She was a busy woman. The sign that something was wrong was her absence at church on Wednesday night. Church wasn't something she missed—even if it meant walking to the highway to catch a ride with a neighbor. Something was definitely wrong. It was then a few neighbors got together, decided to head up to the farmhouse, break a lower window, and see what they might find.

They determined she had been lying there about three days. Not sure if she was alive or had passed, they carried her down the narrow stairs on a stretcher, rushed her to the hospital, and notified the family. Not willing to accept the fact that this vibrant woman was anything but able to bounce back from this setback, we rallied for full medical support for her recovery.

In the Canby nursing home, where we had previously visited grandparents and great aunts, and took cookies to people from church we didn't even know, we watched this vibrant woman diminish to a mere shell of her former self. She had no use of half her body. Her right side, her dominant one, was now useless, making the simple tasks of eating, buttoning a blouse, or opening an envelope, nearly impossible. Walking was out of the question. Rising to the occasion, her left hand took over, but no one would ever say it was easy. She would have to learn everything over.

During the first few years of her nursing home stay, we would bring photo albums from the farm to help with her memory. It also gave us something to talk about because one-sided conversations were always a challenge.

"There's a picture of Dad on the tractor, heading out to the field," we would say. "Mom, remember how he would harvest corn late into the night so we would bring him lunch around three in the afternoon?"

Mom would spread out egg salad sandwiches, cookies, and purple Kool-Aid in a Kerr canning jar. I'm not sure why this memory is so vivid for me today. Maybe it was that my dad worked so hard for the family, or maybe it was because we were all there together, listening to the silence for the few moments the tractor was down. My brother and I would eat as quick as we could so we could start running around like kids do, taking for granted the freedom we had as farm kids.

"Look Mom, here's a picture of Dad and the cows." We raised cattle most of my life, but in their earlier days, Mom talked about raising chickens and selling the eggs for a living.

For me, there was nothing better than a calf whose mother couldn't care for it. Dad would enlist me to be the surrogate mom. I was charged with mixing milk replacer formula and each morning and evening I would make sure the calf drank the appropriate amount. I loved those baby calves. Of course, to people who didn't grow up on a farm, it seemed cruel that eventually that calf would be hauled off to the slaughterhouse. Did it seem cruel back then? Not that I remember. It was our way of life. We were feeding America one calf at a time.

My siblings and I took turns visiting Mom at the home, pushing her to the Dairy Queen, showing her old photos. Slowly her memory got better, her speech expanded, but her right side had abandoned her for good. It was no longer possible to embroider dish towels of a silly duck family for every day of the week. Nor could she make elaborate crafts out of recycled items like an empty spool of thread, some Styrofoam and a piece of yarn with the Just Us Club.

It was a Tuesday when she called me. That wasn't unusual, as we had bought her a phone with five buttons on it. All she had to do was punch the picture of which child she wanted to talk to. "I need you to come on Friday afternoon," she said. Now that was unusual. This was a woman, for as long as I'd known her, had never asked for one thing. She only gave. I was perplexed. I wondered if there might be something wrong. I called my sister Sherry who said she'd be happy to ride along for the three-hour trek to the nursing home.

I don't know that one can love a nursing home, but this place is close. It still wasn't "home" which is where my mom wanted to be, but the advantages of a small Minnesota town nursing home are numerous.

It is situated a block from the church we had attended all our lives. Many people from the congregation took it upon themselves to visit friends and neighbors after church and make a point to visit others as well. They would sit with some who went to our church and some who did not, even if they didn't know them very well. It was what we did. And now people were doing it for me, or, rather, for Mom. All those cookies she baked for the "old people" when she was in her 80's and all the shut-ins she visited with tray favors and crafts were now returning the favor—a visit on Sunday.

Many of the festivities of the small town expanded to the nursing home. It was expected that trick-or-treaters would creep up and down the halls. The prom couples would walk in a grand march formation down every hall, as most of them had grandparents there. And the annual Hat Daze parade would always march or float past the home, knowing all the residents would be lined up in wheelchairs on the curb waiting for candy to be tossed to the crowd. I wish there were more parades.

They also have a golf cart with a large trailer behind it that seats eight wheelchairs at a time. Joe, the activities director, loves taking the residents around town, waving to the locals, pointing out where people live now, or where residents used to live in better days. He takes them past the swimming pool to hear the kids playing and splashing, past the nursery where flowers were started for Mom's gardens. In late July, they stop at the fairgrounds for the county fair and push the residents around for the afternoon. Most of them haven't missed a county fair in fifty years, and they aren't about to miss one now.

But back to Friday, the day Mom wanted us to come. I had to work that morning, so we didn't leave until noon. It was always a treat to leave the city and drive through rolling farmland. It was October, harvest time. As we got to the middle of prairie land, my sister and I opened our windows and breathed in the air, not caring about the dust particles floating into the car. The harvesters were unloading their corn and grain into huge trucks. The farmers would be working late tonight. As a kid, we might have dinner at 10 p.m., if that's when Dad came in from the field. The drive "home" always reminds me of those childhood memories. My husband is quick to point out that "home" is now with him, in the outskirts of The Cities, which is what everyone calls Minneapolis/St Paul. But I know my home will always be in the country, with the endless fields and the quiet of the country.

We arrived at the nursing home at 3 o'clock or so, heading through the front doors, breathing in the smells and sounds of the nursing home, most of them not that pleasant. We headed for Mom's room down the hall on the left, but when we arrived, Connie, the nurse said, "Your mom's not here. Go downstairs and take the hallway to the hospital. That's where you'll find her."

We looked at each other, grimaced a bit, and hurried down the stairs. As we turned the corner to the dreary hallway leading to the hospital, we were greeted by something unexpected. We heard music playing, people talking, and others laughing. Megan, in charge of resident activities, held out a glass of fake champagne. "Welcome to the opening of the Sylvan Court Art Gallery. Our nine artists are seated in front of their paintings and are happy to answer any questions you might have." Then in a lower voice she whispered, "Your mom is on the end."

Somewhat puzzled, we walked down the festive hallway, to see nine women in wheelchairs with works of art decorating the walls. At the end, was Mom.

I still smile when I recall the look of pride on Mom's face as we approached. No longer was she the woman who felt no worth, who struggled with words, who had very little to contribute to the world. Today, she was a confident, proud woman next to the most beautiful painting I had ever seen, done by her left hand. The placard next to it stated, "This was my first work. I wanted to see if I could do it. Lorraine Jesme, Age 90."

Tears filled my eyes as we walked toward Mom and her painting. It was such a surprise. I never imagined she would find a passion at age ninety and unleash such incredible talent. She had never painted before in her life. She wasn't even a particularly creative person. Yes, she made crafts, but mostly they were by following instructions, rather than creating something from scratch. This talent was something we had never seen before. The painting captured a straggly tree having lost its leaves, with the sunset glowing red and low in the sky. It was incredibly beautiful on its own, but more impactful when I realized it symbolized my mother, in the fall of her life.

I will never forget that day. Even at age ninety, she continued to teach life lessons. You are never too old to try something new. And sometimes you will be faced with obstacles that seem impossible to overcome. Try anyway. Put yourself out there. Risk doing something you've never done before, just to see if you can do it.

Tammy Laurent is a financial advisor with 33 years experience, an author and an inspirational speaker. She helps women in sales grow their business, and also helps them feel comfortable on the golf course with prospective clients. She and her husband are co-owners of a golf club in Shakopee, Minnesota. She enjoys playing the piano, and anything outdoors including competing in triathlons, ultra light backpacking, running, swimming, kayaking and golf. She lives with her husband, their border terrier, and their bengal cat in New Prague, Minnesota.

Poison Pie

MIDGE BUBANY

When Lois Filstrom was a girl, she loved playing in her grandmother's attic, smelling of dust, old wood, and times past. She'd learned her family's history from yellowed newspapers, letters, legal documents, and photos she discovered in an antique round-top trunk belonging to her great-great grandparents, Harriet and Bernard Filstrom. She was especially fascinated by old letters from Albert Bowman Rogers to Bernard. Bernard had served in the calvary alongside Rogers in the Dakota uprising in 1862, and Rogers, after leaving the military, became a Milwaukee Railroad engineer. One of his duties was naming towns along the railroad. In the early 1870s, Rogers encouraged Bernard to settle where a new railroad depot was to be located in southern Minnesota, and Rogers honored his friend by naming the town Harrietville after Bernard's wife, Harriet.

Lois now owns the restaurant her ancestors founded just west of the train depot. In one of Rogers' letters, he'd said Harriet's "home-cooked meals and pies were the best he'd tasted in all of Minnesota." Lois's grandmother said it was Harriet's business sense which made their establishments flourish. They also built a hotel and general store, which were eventually sold to extended family, but Harriet's Cafe was kept in the immediate family.

In 1975, Lois, who identified heavily with Harriet, took over not only the popular cafe but also heading Harrietville Founders' Day, renaming it Harriet Days. Under Lois's management, the cafe thrived for forty-plus years, and thanks to her leadership, Harriet Days was a financial boon for the community. The three days of celebration took place the last full week of July. Central Park was the primary site for the food trucks, and activities such as the arts-and-crafts sale, raffle booth, carnival, and the afternoon ice cream social. The baseball tournament, held in Northside Park, ran for the entire three days, while Crazy Daze and the street dance took place on Friday, and the parade on Saturday. Lois planned, organized and prepared for Harriet Days, including having her staff bake all the pies donated for the ice cream social.

The festival ran like a well-oiled machine. . .until it didn't.

The Sunday before Harriet Days, Lois's cousin LeRoy Filstrom, his wife Greta, and their three girls showed up at Harriet's Cafe at noon. This was a surprise because they never so much as bought a cup of coffee from her in the past, even though Lois took her business to their pharmacy. LeRoy inherited the building next door, formerly the Filstrom Hotel, and operated a pharmacy on the ground floor while renting out apartments on the two floors above. During restoration, Filstrom Pharmacy had been stripped of its original charm, but Harriet's Cafe remained a quaint establishment with the original oak booths and handsome counter. The walls displayed maps of early Harrietville and photos of the Filstroms and their businesses. Lois's award-winning cafe was successful because she treated and paid her staff well, and they provided her customers with excellent food and service.

Lois joined the family, and everyone ordered the chicken dinner special. During the meal, Greta, as she tended to do, steered the conversation to local gossip. Bored, the girls were glued to their phones and only chimed in to contradict their mother. After giving the weekly grapevine update, Greta asked, "How's the festival coming?"

"So far so good," Lois said, avoiding giving the gossip queen any fodder.

"It's become too much for you," Greta declared.

Lois forced a smile. "No, I enjoy it."

Greta tossed her a patronizing look. "You should be slowing down at your age. You've been the chairman *forever*, plus you run the restaurant all alone now."

"Everett planting his butt on a stool wasn't much help."

When Greta prompted LeRoy with an elbow to his side, he said, "You should be enjoying life instead of working so hard."

Lois was taken aback. "The festival is important for the community, and I am enjoying my life!"

Greta raised her heavily plucked eyebrows, but she dropped the subject.

On her walk home, Lois chewed on Greta and LeRoy's words: *at your age, chairman forever, too much, run it alone.* Heck, she preferred "alone." Divorcing Everett, her lazy, beer-guzzling, flimflam ex was the best thing she ever did. She was relieved when he moved in with his brother in Mankato, and their encounters would be few. And she wasn't alone. She had her cats, Hawkeye and Trapper, who didn't drink beer or spend her money. Yes, she liked her life: the restaurant gave her a sense of purpose.

The first day of this year's festival ran smoothly. Even the weather cooperated, blessing the festival with a glorious forecast of temperatures in the upper seventies with low humidity. While her staff ran the restaurant, Lois spent much of her time at the park overseeing the festivities, and problem-solving small issues. The whole festival experience gave her joy: smelling the food from the food trucks, hearing band music playing in the background, watching families and friends together at the ice cream social, and seeing the excitement and delighted children at the small carnival. Yes, this festival was important to the community, and she made it happen! But Thursday afternoon, while sipping a strawberry/pine   apple smoothy, Lois experienced a wave of fatigue. Perhaps being chairman was getting to be too much for her.

That night when Lois was walking home, she did a double take when she saw Everett at the wheel of a new red Mercedes convertible. What the...? Did one of his schemes finally pay off? What was he doing in town? Just seeing that lout made Lois's night restless. She hoped he wasn't moving back to town.

Early Friday morning was the first sign of trouble. Lois received a few phone calls from people complaining about mild gastric symptoms after attending the festival. She called the committee together, and after thoroughly discussing the situation, they decided they need not address it.

By Saturday morning, however, it was difficult to ignore the growing list of calls the committee received, so they reconvened. This time they decided to involve Martha Mathers, with the county health department. Martha urged the committee to have the vendors stop selling food but allow them to sell bottled beverages. Lois called Greta to inform her there would be no ice cream social that afternoon. Greta seemed more upset than she was. Martha, being proactive and cautious, also insisted the Minnesota Department of Health be notified.

Disgruntled vendors had to remain until the Department of Health arrived to take samples of food items for testing, which included the pies and ice cream provided by Harriet's Cafe for the social. The nearly fifty individuals with symptoms who came forward were encouraged to go to the hospital to be interviewed and leave "medical samples." Martha said they would be questioned on specific foods and drinks they had consumed in the past forty-eight hours. She also told them the samples collected would be sent to a laboratory, and the results wouldn't be known for some time.

Lois worried this would be the end of Harriet Days—and that she'd be remembered for this year's fiasco and not the decades of successful festivals she'd headed.

Although rumors spread rapidly of a "food-borne illness," many Saturday events carried on at the park but with fewer participants. Elsewhere, Crazy Daze continued—baseball games were played, the afternoon parade traversed the city streets led by the deafening intertwining sirens of two police cars and five firetrucks. Excited children, bags in hand, gathered candy pelted at them from parade units which ranged from farm implements blasting horns loud enough to wake the dead in the cemetery two miles out of town, to the mediocre high school band, a drum and bugle corps group, a local country band on a flatbed trailer, and troops of youthful gymnasts and scouts. Lois's favorite unit was the Chamber of Commerce float which carried the Harriet and Bernard costume contest winners. People were having fun. Not all was lost.

By Saturday evening only a thin crowd gathered to listen to the local band, and by closing time only a handful of people were in front of the stage when the raffle contest winners were announced. And just like that, the festival was over in what felt like a puff of defeat.

Lois tossed and turned all night, pondering what could have caused the illnesses. Did someone sabotage the festival? But why would someone do that? She was so worried about preserving her family's legacy with Harriet Days, she didn't consider at that point the restaurant could also be in peril.

During Sunday's breakfast run, Lois heard the rumors her pies were the source of the mystery illness. "Poison pie," they said. For the next two weeks, the restaurant's profits were down fifty percent, but to Lois's relief, business gradually picked up, even pie sales.

On the third Monday in August, Martha Mathers dropped by in the afternoon.

"Our results came back quickly. There's no evidence of any food-borne illness," Martha said as she handed Lois a copy of the report.

"What?" Lois said.

"It's not that surprising since the symptoms were so mild," Martha said.

"What was it then? Some virus?"

"More likely a substance found its way into the food."

"Found its way? Like purposefully?"

"Or accidentally. Mistakes happen. Whatever, it wasn't lethal. I have an employee finishing up crosschecking what the victims consumed. Now, I best go. I promised the newspaper editor, Dan Vogel, I'd report to him the results as soon as they were available."

When the paper came out, Lois was disappointed in the teeny article on the second page. *The test results couldn't pinpoint the cause, but the festival leadership should be applauded for preventing more illness.* Yippy skippy.

The next Sunday LeRoy and Greta invited Lois for an evening barbecue, a rare invitation.

After Greta's gossip update, Lois said, "I saw Everett driving a Mercedes convertible in town."

Greta's wine glass stopped midway to her mouth. She looked to LeRoy.

"Did you talk to him?" Greta asked.

"No, he just drove by."

"Good, you don't want him back, do you?" Greta asked.

"Why? Because he's driving a fancy car? I'm not a teenager and had too many decades of watching him sit in his recliner for hours, drinking twelve-packs, and thinking of ways to throw money he never earned at worthless business schemes!"

"At least he tried to make it a go of it," LeRoy said.

"Are you serious?" Lois asked.

"He was always friendly to me," LeRoy said.

"Yes, the man could talk a leg off a three-legged dog," said Lois.

LeRoy waited until after dinner was served (ribs slathered with Lois's signature barbecue sauce recipe, corn on the cob, and coleslaw) to drop a bombshell. "We want to buy Harriet's."

It took a few seconds for Lois to register his words. "What? Why?"

"To keep it in the family," LeRoy said.

Lois stared at the couple. They wanted her cafe?

"Harriet's has become too much for you, and with the disaster Harriet Days was, your business has surely suffered," Greta said.

"It's rebounded, but it wasn't anything I did or didn't do," Lois said.

"Wasn't it?" Greta said. "We think you're burnt out."

Lois' hackles raised. "What's really going on?"

"Think about retiring," LeRoy said. "You're seventy-two fer cryin' out loud."

"Seventy-one," Lois corrected.

Greta giggled, her chubby checks rosy from four glasses of white Zinfandel she'd consumed. "For you, I would step aside from the ice cream social to take over the chairmanship. Then you could enjoy the fun without the work."

"For me, huh?" Lois said. No, Greta wanted to take charge and they wanted her cafe.

"Well, I'd be surprised if Harriet Days wasn't cancelled next year given everyone got sick from your poisoned pies," Greta said.

"My pies were not poisoned. Martha said it could have been a substance accidentally put into the vendor food or beverages."

LeRoy grunted. "Where'd she come up with that one?"

"Maybe it was in the flour you used for your pie crust. That happens," said Greta.

"Or someone put something in a beverage. Someone with an ulterior motive," Lois offered.

Greta laughed. "Careful, you sound paranoid."

At that moment, Lois hated them both for not supporting her. She claimed she had a headache and left.

LeRoy and Greta's pitch to buy her out was disturbing and insulting.

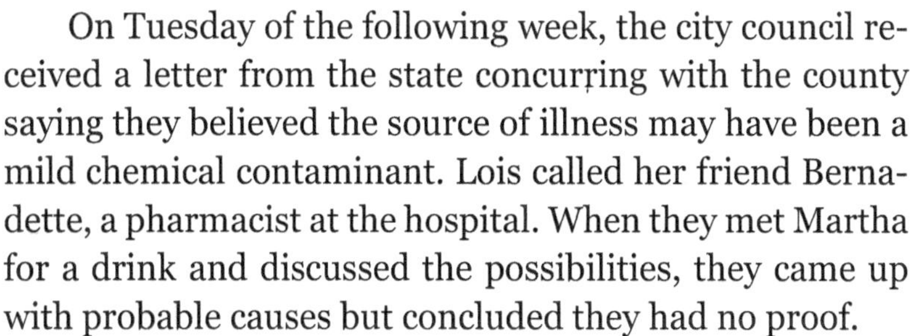

On Tuesday of the following week, the city council received a letter from the state concurring with the county saying they believed the source of illness may have been a mild chemical contaminant. Lois called her friend Bernadette, a pharmacist at the hospital. When they met Martha for a drink and discussed the possibilities, they came up with probable causes but concluded they had no proof.

On Thursday, real estate agent Jackie Morris dropped by the restaurant with an anonymous offer to buy Harriet's Cafe.

Jackie was a nice person, so Lois didn't wish to be rude. She smiled when she firmly said, "Harriet's is not for sale."

"Don't you want to hear the offer?"

"Nope."

"All right, I will tell my buyers."

"You do that."

After Jackie left, Lois growled out LeRoy and Greta's names.

When Lois arrived at the restaurant early the next morning, Deedee, a veteran wait staffer, said she just caught Greta back by the coffee pot. "She slipped something in her pocket when she saw me and now the coffee smells funny."

"Did you say anything to her?"

"I asked if I could help her. She said she'd come back later."

"The cameras should have picked it up," Lois said.

Lois replayed the video and then called Bernadette, her pharmacist friend. Bernadette told Lois to bring in a coffee sample, then clean and sanitize the pots. An hour later, Lois had her results. The coffee was laced with syrup of ipecac, which induces vomiting.

Bernadette said, "As we discussed earlier, I believe a tasteless, powdered laxative could have been added to the coffee at the festival because Martha said in reviewing the cross-checking, the only thing those who had symptoms consumed in common was the coffee at the ice cream social."

"Greta's ice cream social." Lois said.

"Can't prove it now, but you can prove what went down today," Bernadette said.

Lois, Bernadette, and Martha met with Police Chief Ken Johnson, and together they came up with a plan of action.

Lois called Jackie and arranged a meeting at Harriet's after closing on Saturday with the party who offered the bid to buy the restaurant. As predicted, Jackie arrived with Greta and LeRoy, and Lois seated them in the back room.

Then on cue, in walked Bernadette, Martha, and Chief Johnson. The couple looked confused, concerned. Then in burst Everett, wearing his standard uniform: a ratty band T-shirt, jean shorts, and a baseball cap. Lois was stunned.

"Sorry, I'm late," he said, and went to shake LeRoy's hands.

"You're in on this, Everett? Did you finally strike gold?" Lois asked.

"Sorta. My brother, Norman, died. He left me quite well off," Everett said with a smirk.

Lois's heart sunk. She liked Norman. Everett had his father's good looks, but Norman was kind and responsible, and that's why he'd inherited the family farm in the first place. Now, Everett had Norman's hard-earned money and revenge in his heart. Lois was heartbroken her family would consort with Everett but would particularly enjoy what was about to unfold.

Chief Johnson said, "Everyone sit." They all silently stared at the large man in the uniform. "I'll cut to the chase. The only people who got sick at the festival had coffee at the ice cream social, and that's not a coincidence."

Greta and LeRoy's faces dropped. Everett sat back in his chair and crossed his arms over his chest.

"We suspect a tasteless laxative was added to the coffee, but since Greta quickly dumped it, it couldn't be tested." But we do have proof she poured ipecac in the cafe's coffee. Contaminating food is a gross misdemeanor and has serious legal consequence like a fine, imprisonment."

Greta sputtered, "I did not pour . . ."

"Caught you on tape," the Chief said. "I suspect you two want to buy out Lois to bolster your failing pharmacy business. Everett, I don't know what your deal is."

LeRoy stood. "Offer's withdrawn. Let's go, Greta," he said.

"I don't think so," said the Chief. "At least not Greta. Although I suspect you two dolts were complicit, I'm just taking Greta in tonight."

"I never thought you three would sink so low," Lois said. "It was you who spread the poison-pie rumor. Turns out it's you who've been poisoned by greed."

LeRoy and Everett watched Chief Johnson handcuff Greta, read her the Miranda Rights, and lead her out to the squad; then they bolted.

Unfortunately for them, Greta sung like a canary during interrogation. The men, both hungover, were arrested early the next morning at LeRoy's. According to Greta, the plan hatched after the couple saw Norman's obituary and attended his funeral. They knew Everett would have inherited cash he could invest. With the pharmacy struggling, LeRoy and Greta were jealous of Lois's success and saw her popular restaurant as a cash cow. The two of them devised the scheme, not Everett.

Months later, a sheriff's notice of a foreclosure was posted on the pharmacy door. Lois approached her staff about forming a company together and buying the building. With the city's help, the first floor was converted to a senior citizen's center with a space for the Harrietville Museum. Since she considered her staff her family, her latest will named them as her only benefactors. When Lois retired at eighty-eight, Deedee took over management of both Harriet's and Harriet Days and both are still thriving.

The most popular pie at Harriet's continues to be Lois's Badass Blueberry.

Midge Bubany is the author of four published police-procedural mystery novels set in north central Minnesota and four short stories in anthologies. Midge has studied writing at the Loft Literary Center and has educated herself on police procedures using several resources, including attending the Orono Citizens Police Academy and the Hennepin County Sheriff's Law Enforcement Citizens Academy. She is a member of Women of Words and the Twin Cities Sisters in Crime. Midge lives with her dog, Juni, in the western suburbs of Minneapolis.

STORY 21

A Restless Winter

ALANA FAULK

Snowflakes drifted from the anemic sky, placing a wet chill in the air that reached inside of Sydney's woolen, winter coat, making her bones ache. Pulling her soft, red scarf tighter around her flushed cheeks, she trudged through the pristine, white snow that had drifted across her driveway during the night. Shivering as she brushed the bothersome slush from her Mercedes, she sighed as she was finally able to slip inside the car and start the engine. As the luxurious sedan purred and came to life, she flipped on the seat warmers and cranked the heat up to full capacity. Sydney then scrambled back out into the January wind to finish the incessant task of brushing and scraping her way through the rest of this year's dreary, disheartening Minnesota winter.

It was part of a wearisome, daily ritual which had somehow, sadly, come to define her colorless, humdrum life. Every day, she rose before the sun, showered, and then downed a cup and a half of very strong, very black coffee. She then proceeded to inch her way down I-394 in a zombie-like state until she drove up the exit to the Richfield Plastic plant. Heading straight for the time clock,

Sydney would unenthusiastically punch in while mentally preparing to face another long shift of counting the minutes as they ticked past, while doing a job she hated more than anything else in life.

Sydney lived for her afternoon lunch break, when she would hide in a quiet corner of the huge break room with a bag of chips and an ice-cold Coca Cola. Taking full advantage of this gift of personal time, she would immerse herself into the life of the main character of whatever novel she was engrossed in that week. It was the best hour of the day, and sadly, passed the quickest. She had always loved to read. Books were her passion, and she could not even venture to guess how many she had devoured through the years. She imagined it must have been thousands. Before taking the dreadful job at Richfield, she had spent her days working at the Maple Grove Public Library. For Sydney, it had been a dream job, getting paid to surround herself with shelves upon shelves of glorious books, and spending her life just an arm's length away from the magnificent words of the world's finest authors. Walking into the building gave her great joy every morning as the rich scent of the leather-bound classics mingled with the aroma of the fresh newsprint of the *New York Times* and *The Wall Street Journal*. The most amazing part of her job was her privilege to read, at her leisure, any books she chose during down time and slow periods. She had made it her purpose to read a book from a different section of the library every few days and relished in the reality that her choices were perpetual and infinite. The library became her home away from home and she loved just being there. The only problem with her job was the pay had been nominal—awful, in fact—with her earning just a smidge more than minimum wage. Despite her small paycheck, she still considered this to be the best job of all time and can still recall the sense of heartbreak she had felt on her last day working there.

"Richfield Plastic is hiring!" her best friend, Carly, had told her. "It's the first time in nearly ten years!" The news had, in fact, been the talk of the town. Rumor had it that starting pay was $18 an hour, with full benefits and guaranteed overtime, not to mention a substantial raise after a year. Sydney had rushed to the plant to fill out an application along with half of the county and was more than a bit surprised when she received a call to come in for an interview. The man behind the desk studied her application and asked a few questions, but Sydney had nearly fallen out of her chair when he told her to report for work on Monday morning—she was hired! She left the building with her head spinning as she thought about paying off all of her debts. She would be able to afford a townhouse in a better neighborhood and as she walked to the very back of the parking lot, where she had hidden her rusted-out Chevy, Sydney promised herself a new car.

In preparation for her first day of training, Sydney had bought a new outfit for herself. She was excited to make a good first impression but was very disappointed when her supervisor handed her a Richfield Plastics uniform upon walking in the door. It was the smallest size they carried but since it was made for a man, it hung off her body like the flannel shirt on Uncle Pete's scarecrow. She would have shuddered had she known she would spend most of the next eight years in one of those hideous uniforms.

The days only got worse from there. The job was tedious, the shift was long, and she drove home exhausted most nights. Believing it would get better, Sydney returned day after dreary day, until she found herself, nearly a decade later, still punching into the same old tired timeclock, seeing the same weary faces, and living the same dull and lonely life. Where had all of the years gone? Looking back, she had no real memories, friends, or loved ones. Yes, she drove an expensive car...to work and back. She lived in a swanky new apartment in the very desirable Lakeview Estates, though all she ever seemed to do there was laundry and sleep. Her bank account had grown substantially over time, as had her 401K account after many years of sixty-hour work weeks, raises, and overtime. Sydney's home was full of all of the latest and greatest newfangled gadgets and full of costly furniture, yet with all of this stuff, she still lived an empty, lonesome life. Friends and family had stopped calling long ago since she was never home and when she was, she was too exhausted to entertain or socialize. Nope, this was not the life Sydney had hoped for. She longed for the simple existence she had once enjoyed—the quiet refuge of her library, the books, the stories and most of all, the freedom to dream.

Gloomy, Sydney headed up the exit ramp while the snow continued to tumble from the sky. Upon reaching the plant, she heaved a heavy sigh as she rolled through the towering steel gates. With a dark mood and a sinking heart, she pulled into a parking space. Staring at the massive, red brick building that loomed ominously before her, she felt her head begin to swim as a surge of nausea filled her throat. Cascades of snow began to envelope the car. The flakes melted quickly on the warm windshield, running swiftly down the glass, and still she remained, sedentary and sullen. Reaching for the ignition, she frowned and then let her hand drop into her lap as she sank back into the rich leather seat of the idling Mercedes. With her mind racing, she sat in silence and contemplated her future. In her mind's eye, she envisioned living the same lonely life, working the same monotonous job, day after dismal day, where she would eventually wither up and grow old before her time.

At that precise moment, something transpired—a thought, a wish, a notion; she could not be sure. Considering her future, Sydney suddenly understood the existence she was immersed in was not living, it was dying. This plant, this place—this *job*—stole one precious day from her limited allotment every single time she passed through these gates. Today, the nightmare would end, and her intended life would begin. Realizing she had paid her dues and sacrificed priceless years of her life, she cultivated a plan. Somewhere out there, in a charming, coastal town, there was a quaint little bookstore for sale. Sydney would collect her hard-earned money, pack up her things, and go find it. Once located, she would set up shop, getting to know the folks and history of her new community. There would be a delightful little house near the water with a white picket fence, a porch swing, and a flower garden. In this place she would grow much more than roses and tulips; she would let her spirit flourish, as well.

Sydney still stared at the factory before her, but for the first time in a very long time, she smiled. As she reached out and shifted the car into reverse, she was overcome with an intense feeling of both relief and excitement. As she maneuvered her car back out through those imprisoning gates, she resisted the urge to call her supervisor, thinking to herself, *No call, no show, no turning back.*

Alana Marie is a Minnesota author, whose tales and yarns are based on actual events that have occurred throughout her very colorful life. Some of the stories may revolve around the trials and tribulations of friends and family but all include some shred of truth. Alana, herself, is an out and proud lesbian who once weighed 528 pounds. A former bar and nightclub owner with a serious infatuation for food and alcohol, she has overcome tremendous obstacles throughout the years. Now sober for more than a decade, she has published two books on Amazon under *the Pick a Struggle Cupcake* title. Alana has also been published in *Chicken Soup for the Soul* and *WW Thin-line magazine*. In sharing experiences and recovery in a raw, yet sensitive fashion, she hopes to inspire, provoke and motivate others to take the steps necessary to chase their dreams and conquer their own demons and dilemmas. Enjoy her stories and struggles...they come from the heart.

SCAVENGER HUNT
Lynn Garthwaite

When I began this scavenger hunt, I didn't expect it to almost kill me. It sounded like fun, and when I created one for my friend Carly, I had her scavenger hunt take her to places where she'd see penguins (at The Como Park Zoo), could get an iced latte (at Spyhouse Coffee), and enjoy a sunset banjo concert (at the Lake Harriet bandshell). In total I sent her to five different places around the Twin Cities, hiding my clues in places that not only would be relatively easy to find, but give her fun things to do while she was there.

But dear, evil-minded Carly had something else in mind when it was her turn to send me on a hunt. The only rules we had established were the clues 1) had to be hidden someplace within the metro area of Minneapolis and St. Paul, and 2) be accessible. We should have spent more time defining the word "accessible."

My first clue arrived at my door by way of bicycle courier. I live in a condo in downtown Minneapolis because I'm single, like to walk to restaurants, football games, the theater…and because what 27-year-old single woman wouldn't want to live on the 12th floor of a downtown condo? The clue was delivered in a bright pink envelope that pretty much screamed "Carly," so I suspected the hunt was on. When I wrote a set of clues for her last week, it took her four hours to find the prize, which was a deck of playing cards with a dragon motif. My plan was to beat that time and have some bragging rights.

I tipped the bike guy, who was kind of cute, by the way. Oh golly, just look at him walk away. But the hunt! I couldn't wait to start the hunt! Did she seal the envelope with SuperGlue or something? Two paper cuts later, I was staring at a piece of paper in the shape of a...what was it? A brain or something? Maybe a liver? Carly is just a little bit crazy.

And such a smart-ass. Carly typed the clues in the font we always shared jokes about. "Who would ever use this smomo font?" we'd ask. "Smomo" was the secret word that Carly and I used whenever we wanted to make fun of something without letting anyone else know that's what we were doing. "Smomo car, Miles. Love those head-lights." "Where did you get those smomo sandals, Tiff?"

So, in the smomoiest of fonts, Carly's first clue was right there in front of me.

CHUTE THE LADDER, OR CHUTE THE BREEZE

It didn't take me long to figure out where the clue led. I thought I was pretty brilliant but then I realized she made it too easy. Chutes and Ladders is a kids' ingeniously giant playground in Bloomington. Just last week Carly had her five-year-old niece for the day, and the two of us took her to the playground first and then swam at nearby Bush Lake. We joked that the kids there were "chuting" slides while we shot the breeze. Genius wordsmiths, Carly and I.

I put on my shoes and hit "start" on the app that was going to allow Carly to follow my progress through my phone. In the same way, I had followed her progress last week, with the idea that if we saw the other person going around in circles we'd call and give them a fresh clue to put them on the right path. But Carly's little clues looked like they were going to be easy, and I should be able to cut her time in half.

It turned out Carly had no intention of making it easy. I was lucky that today was a school day because it meant that only a few kids were climbing the ladders and rocketing down the enormous slides. What were they doing there anyway? Had they called in sick? When I do that it's because I want to be at the movie theater on opening day for a new Chris Pratt film.

I looked around and realized that I actually did have my work cut out for me. The place had roughly eight billion places to hide a clue. The supposedly-sick kids were on some of the equipment, so I figured I'd start where they weren't, and that took me to a series of low-to-the-ground pieces of climbing stuff meant for the little tots. I'll spare you the details, but it was actually an hour later, after I'd covered almost every square inch of that entire thousand-acre (okay, maybe two-acre) play area, that I spotted a little piece of something pink poking out between a signpost and a fence.

It was not even *in* the playground area, but rather over by the building that housed bathrooms and, presumably, first aid equipment to treat children who fall from climbing equipment.

Carly was more devious than I gave her credit for. Now I knew to start looking in the less-obvious places and sure enough, her next clue was a little harder. The smomo font read:

IT STICKS OUT.
DON'T BE ALL
DRAMATIC AND FALL

Initially, I couldn't imagine what the clue meant, so I stopped for an ICEE at the gas station. One giant brain-freeze later, my mind started working again, and I realized she was talking about the Guthrie Theater. Downtown Minneapolis. *Downtown.* Where I had started the day almost two hours ago. So that meant she sent me into the suburbs for the first clue, and then back downtown, six blocks from my condo, for the second. She could have had me *start* downtown. Why had I never noticed this sociopathic side of Carly before?

The Guthrie Theater is one of the centerpieces of downtown Minneapolis, and it has a very unique cantilevered "bridge" that juts out 178 feet from the main building. The view of downtown is cool, but it's from a place in which you imagine you may be seconds away from plunging 55 feet to your death. We'd been to plays together, and Carly always said when I walk into that building I suddenly start speaking with an English accent and get "all dramatic." The clue made sense.

Parking downtown on a weekday can make me break out in hives, so I pulled into my own parking spot at my condo, hoofed it six blocks to the Guthrie, and went inside. The feel of that place, the drama, the suspense, all begins when you walk into the lobby. But today I didn't have time to dwell on it. I was up against a clock, so I hit the stairs to get up to the level that opened to the cantilevered bridge. I couldn't imagine where she could hide a clue, however. There aren't any nooks or crannies to wedge a piece of paper. No obscure corners or hanging drapes. I wandered the length of the bridge, trying to tamp down the part of my brain that was yelling *Get off this bridge. Can't you see there is nothing underneath holding it up? Are you even sure what 'cantilevered' means?*

I found nothing on the bridge. When I made my way back to the main foyer, a man in an odd costume that looked like a cross between a peacock and a weasel (trust me, you have to see it), approached me, made a very impressive sweeping bow, and whipped a pink envelope from some part of his weasel, while dramatically delivering the words "I believe you dropped this, madam."

He handed me the envelope and, without a word, disappeared through a door.

Oh boy, that girl is GOOD. She completely put my pathetic little scavenger hunt to shame. How did she plan all of this? I guessed that she sent a signal to the peacock/weasel guy when she saw on the GPS app that I had arrived at the Guthrie Theater, but did she know him? Did she hire him? I couldn't wait for the conversation we were going to have at the end of the hunt.

The next clue was more smomo:

It's Not The Time Of Year For Christmas Cacti

Long story short, she was sending me to the Como Park Conservatory, steps away from where I sent her last week to the Como Park Zoo. The Conservatory contains a lush bounty of gorgeous flowering plants, which is especially delightful when it's the middle of winter and you can walk inside and see and smell all of the plants that you take for granted in the summer. Dahlias in June are just another beautiful flower. But seeing them in December makes you swoon with delight.

And she was right. This is not the time of year for Christmas cacti because it was the beginning of September, and summer flowers were still in bloom around town.

To summarize the things that my sociopathic friend put me through by the third hour: I spent an hour climbing up and down the playground equipment at Chutes and Ladders, drove back downtown and repressed my fear of falling at the Guthrie Theater, scratched myself pulling a pink envelope out from behind an especially prickly cactus at the Como Park Conservatory (I wasn't supposed to touch the plants, but she hid it there. What could I do?), and then followed up by having to shinny up a tree at Theodore Wirth Park.

From that envelope I pulled the last clue:

You Can See It From The Front Any Time Of Year, But From The Back Only In Winter

If I was going to beat Carly's time of four hours on the hunt I designed for her last week, I was going to have to really hustle. But I couldn't figure out what the clue meant. Coming from Theodore Wirth Park, I was already all the way in the northern suburb of Golden Valley, so I started driving south, figuring that wherever that clue led was going to at least be in this direction. I stopped for a burger and fries to help my brain think.

Finally, it dawned on me. Minnehaha Falls, right in the heart of beautiful Minneapolis. The falls flow about nine months of the year, but for the other three months they freeze up, creating an amazingly beautiful piece of art. The frozen ice forms a thick curtain from the bridge where the water drops to where it meets up with the rest of Minnehaha creek below.

In the winter, adventurous and, sure, sometimes intoxicated people like to climb down to the frozen creek and then scurry up and behind the frozen ice curtain so that they are, in essence, behind the falls. It's all rock back there, both under foot and behind them, and icy conditions create a problem for people crawling around. Especially for the intoxicated ones. Sometimes rescue squads have to be called in, and that's why it's actually illegal to do that. But it doesn't mean that people don't.

So, with my brilliant and well-fed brain checking the clock, I headed to where Minnehaha Drive meets up with 46th street and went to the park where my family spent years picnicking, hiking, viewing the falls, and even hosting some big family get-togethers in the giant pavilion. I could hear the falls roaring when I got close, the creek overflowing, no doubt because of the heavy rains this summer. The stone walls that accented all areas of the park had been built during the Great Depression under FDR's New Deal initiative, and all these years later they were still beautiful and sturdy; they spoke of a time when people pulled together to just survive.

I never tire of this beautiful park and those falls. I wanted to stand on the bridge where you can look down at the point where the creek crashes and violently hits the floor below, but I needed to get to Carly's final clue. I hoped she hid it near the falls because the rest of the park was huge, and it could take a week to find it. Her clue specifically mentioned looking at the falls, so I started down the 108 steps that would bring me to the bottom where the water from the falls continued along the creek for miles.

Halfway down the stairs I thought my eye caught on something in the water. It was pink, but *in* the water? Why would Carly do that? As I continued down the steps, I could see that the pink envelope was not actually in the water, but rather somehow stuck on a rock or piece of wood in the creek. It looked like I was going to get wet.

When I hit the bottom of the steps, I crossed the little bridge to the side of the creek where there is a walking path that goes through woods and along the creek for miles. I'd walked it many times, but at that moment I was trying to keep my eye on that pink envelope.

I squeezed between a couple of giant boulders and then ended up on a flat, sandy area where the sides of the creek lapped up. There, about six feet into the water, and not far from where the falls were slamming down, was a pink envelope sitting on a large boulder, with another, smaller rock sitting on top of the envelope, holding it in place.

Yes, I was definitely going to get wet. I slipped off my sandals but then realized that the jeans I was wearing were those slim ones that hug your legs all the way down to your ankles. There is no way to roll them up, and I sure wasn't going to strip right here in public. So, I carefully stepped into the water, my feet immediately seizing up because I hadn't expected the water to be so cold. We'd just had a really nice, warm summer, and all of the lakes were of that perfect swimming temperature, but not this creek. I gasped as I took a second step, calculating how far I'd have to go before I could reach the envelope.

Three steps in and the water was already up to my calves. The wet denim was sucked up tight against my skin. There was definitely no turning back now, and my only consolation was knowing that Carly had to have experienced this same ice-cold trek in order to plant the clue. Two more steps. No, it was going to take three. Now the water was up to my knees, and I suddenly felt my feet slipping out from under me. I started swinging my arms like a windmill, trying to hold my balance, but it was no use.

I was down on my butt, with water swirling around me. Now I was mad, and even more determined. I half crawled the rest of the way and grabbed at the envelope.

At first it wouldn't give, because the rock on top of it was hefty, but that rock wasn't going to beat the determination of a wet, cold, pretty-angry-but-even-more-determined woman, because I only had ten minutes on the clock if I was going to beat Carly's time.

One great tug and I felt the rock tip, just enough so I could pull that damned pink envelope out, and then turn around and start slogging my way back to the sand. The only parts of me that were dry were my boobs, my shoulders, and my head.

Grabbing my sandals, I walked back to the short bridge and then to the 108 steps that seemed absurdly harder to climb now that I was sopping wet. Eventually I emerged at the top and took a moment to lean against the stone wall. I fought to get my sandals back on over my wet feet, and then opened the envelope. Inside was Carly's final message:

Was That a Rocky Road, Or Is Your Rocky Road Starting To Melt?

I tried to stay mad, but I couldn't. I looked up to see Carly sitting at one of the tables outside of the pavilion, holding up a towel and pointing to a bowl of rocky road ice cream. I'm totally going to get her next time, but first I'm going for that ice cream.

Lynn Garthwaite is the author of eleven books, including the *Dirkle Smat Adventure* book series, three picture books for clients (Radio Flyer and Shutterfly), and an historic non-fiction for all ages titled *Our States Have Crazy Shapes: Panhandles, Bootheels, Knobs and Points*. She has also written a mystery/thriller: *Starless Midnight* and an updated nursery rhyme book titled *Childhood Rhymes for Modern Times*. *Your Children Can be Writers: 40 Story Prompts to Spark their Creative Genius* was released in 2022. Lynn is also a copyeditor for three magazines and a publisher, and a member of Sisters in Crime.

A Second Chance

GLORIA FREDKOVE

I t seems like a lifetime ago since I was happily married. *You Light Up My Life* was our wedding song. I still love the song, but our marriage ended after 20 years. Finding a man at my age is like trying to find gold in a jar full of gumballs. I have the worst luck on the internet. Men say they're tall, and when I meet them, they're shorter than I am. I'm 5'4" with heels on. My best friend, Bea, who was also divorced, got lucky on the internet and is re-married now.

I'm not surprised that it was Bea who got lucky. She's tall, attractive, and has long, auburn hair. She applies her eye makeup perfectly, accentuating her sky-blue eyes. I'm short and average-looking. Wearing lipstick makes me look like Ronald McDonald.

I think Bea feels sorry for me. She's always finding new stores and restaurants to show me. She actually convinced me to go with her to the Mall of America tomorrow. I've never been there since it opened in 1992. Can you believe it? It's got over 500 retail stores, an indoor amusement park, restaurants, an aquarium, and just about anything you could want. I doubt they have the one thing I want more than anything else: a man who is available!

⁂

"There's one." I was beginning to think we'd never find a parking spot. Bea takes a picture of the parking locator sign: F 5. I have to admit, I'm excited. The mall is bigger than I imagined. As we make our way inside, I feel oddly like a tourist myself. There are delicate chandeliers hanging overhead with rows of small, soft lights. I smell the fresh-brewed coffee at the Caribou we pass. Unfortunately, I can't drink coffee. Naturally, everywhere I go there are a dozen versions of coffee drinks. And now I smell popcorn, which I can't eat because I always get some stuck in my teeth. God, this place is huge. Was this a good idea?

Look at that roller coaster! It's as loud as thunder, faster than your eyes can follow, and the kids are screaming for their lives. As we're navigating our way around, I see young families, couples, and teenagers who look like they forgot to get dressed. Bea takes me into one store after another. It's fun discovering all these stores, but I'm overwhelmed and tired. We explore the second and third levels. Feels like we've been walking for hours.

"You look tired, Donna. Should we take a break and have lunch?"

"Sure," I say, trying not to fall over.

"Let's go up to the food court. There are lots of choices, so we can each get what we want."

"Sounds good to me." A nap sounds even better.

It feels *so* good to sit down. We're both eating salads, and we share an order of fries.

"So, Donna. What do you think? Isn't this place amazing?"

Bea looks so pleased with herself, like she's just shown me the Eiffel Tower.

"Oh, I can't wait to come back!" Actually, I don't care if I ever see this place again.

"I knew you'd love it, Donna. You can get just about anything you want here. It's great! What do you think about the indoor amusement park?"

"It's okay, I guess," I say, trying not to encourage her.

"I think it's great for the kids. They can go on rides all year because everything's indoors. We have to come back so I can show you the rest of the mall."

"Only if I'm on roller skates! You know, this place actually reminds me of Manhattan. I don't regret moving here years ago, but a little piece of my heart is still in New York."

"Excuse me, ladies, did one of you just mention New York?"

I look up to see a handsome man around my age. Where did he come from? He's tall, handsome and reminds me of George Clooney. Love his green eyes. My cheeks suddenly feel flushed.

"Yes, I'm from New York," I say, raising the pitch of my voice in an effort to sound young.

"What a lovely coincidence. I'm from New York, too. Did you live right in the city?"

"Yes. Near Gramercy Park. Do you know where that is?"

"I sure do. My office wasn't too far from there. Manhattan's great. It's where all the action is, right?" He winks at me. My cheeks are burning and I'm sure they're red. I haven't felt this way since college. He looks deep into my eyes as if there's a prize inside. I think I'm in love!

"I'm actually from Brooklyn, but my practice brought me into the city every day. I've been here about three months now, and I love it." Oh, good, he's not a tourist.

"Do you live close by?"

"I live in Bloomington, so yes, pretty close, but I still get lost occasionally."

Bea can tell that I'm falling for this guy. She gives me a knowing smile and excuses herself. Bea, you're the best!

"Mind if I sit down until your friend comes back?" he asks.

"Not at all. Be my prince...I mean, be my guest. I'm Donna. And you are ...?"

"Donna, it's my pleasure!" He extends his hand to shake mine. "I'm Michael. Some of my friends call me Mike, but I prefer Michael."

"I love the name Michael," I say. "It sounds biblical." What is wrong with me? I'm babbling.

He smiles again, and for the first time, I notice that he has perfect teeth. Wonder if they're real or dental implants?

"So, Donna, what brought you to Minnesota?"

"Oh, my former husband grew up in Minneapolis."

"I see. My wife died a year ago."

"Oh, I'm sorry to hear that." Great, he's single.

"Thank you. It helps to be in a new environment. There's nothing like this mall in New York. Do you shop here often?"

"Actually, this is my first time here, and I've lived here for 30 years."

"Well, I love it. I get my exercise and shopping done at the same time."

"That's a great idea. I'll have to try that the next time I'm here."

"Oh, darn––I just remembered I'm meeting someone in ten minutes. Could I call you sometime? Maybe we could have dinner?"

"I'd like that." I take a card from my purse and hand it to him.

"Thanks. I'll call you soon, Donna. It was a pleasure meeting you." It's obvious he's crazy about me.

As he rushes off, I notice Bea heading back to the table. Perfect timing.

"I just gave Michael my card. God, I hope he calls. He's a widower. Do you know what that means?"

"What?"

"It means he's *available*!"

It's been three whole days, and I haven't heard from Michael. Why do men take your phone number and never call? I'm sick of living alone. I'm sick of Netflix and Prime Video. I'm tired of looking for love on the internet. Michael is perfect for me.

Oh, there goes my phone. Please, God, let it be him.

"Hello?"

"Hi, it's Bea."

"Oh, hi."

"What's wrong? You sound depressed."

"You could say that. I haven't heard from Michael. I knew it was too good to be true."

"It's only been a few days, Donna. Give the guy a chance. Besides, you don't really know anything about him, do you?"

"Well, we both come from New York, he's been in Minnesota for three months, and he lives in Bloomington. And the last thing is I can't stop thinking about him."

"Listen. There's an exhibit of Native American art at the Minneapolis Institute of Art. It looks really good. Want to go?"

"Why not? Maybe I'll fall in love with a painting!"

"I'll pick you up around ten tomorrow morning. Oh, and bring a sweater. It's only May, but they might have their air conditioning on, and you're always freezing."

"Thanks for reminding me. See you tomorrow."

<hr>

We're one of the first ones to arrive. I look outside and notice more people are starting to trickle in. Being here has improved my mood. Minnesota has so much to offer. I love it here. I love going to the Guthrie, or Orchestra Hall, but I haven't been to either place in ages. I'd go out a lot more if I had someone special in my life to share the culture with.

Before we see the exhibit, Bea needs her coffee so we sit down at a snack area. I get to watch her enjoy her latte.

Oh, my God! Is that who I think it is? He looks just like Michael. What the heck? He's walking by with someone half his age. What does she have that I don't, besides youth, beautiful hair and a great figure? This is embarrassing. I hope he doesn't see me.

Bea recognizes him, and before I can say anything, she waves him over.

"Good morning, ladies, how nice to see you again. This is my daughter, Emily."

"Nice to meet you, Emily." His daughter? Thank you, God.

"Emily, these are the two lovely ladies I met at the Mall of America the other day."

"Hi!" She's almost as tall as her father. I bet she's smart like him, too.

"Emily is here to explore the Twin Cities. She's an art major at NYU. I think she'd love it here."

Bea says, "Minnesota is great, except it can get pretty cold in the winter." That's a bit of an understatement.

Emily brushes her long, blonde hair away from her eyes, which are the same color as Michael's. "I thought I'd stay with dad for a while. He's been lonely since Mom died." She's beautiful. Wish she'd go back to New York.

"Oh, I'm so sorry to hear that." I could change that in an instant if he'd give me a chance!

"Well," says, Michael, "We better head out to the exhibit. We're meeting some friends for lunch. Oh ... Donna?"

"Yes?"

He bends down and whispers in my ear. "I have your card right inside my wallet. I'll call you just as soon as I get Emily settled. I'd love to take you to dinner."

"Sounds good, Michael." He's walking away too quickly. I know he'll call, but how long do I have to wait?

"Donna, come back to earth! Don't you see you're rushing things?"

"No, I don't. I can tell from the way Michael looked at me that just now that he's attracted to me. He just needs a little encouragement. What a great coincidence we both wound up here today. Oh, Bea, this is serendipity. This is my chance!"

"What do you mean?"

"I'll be right back. Don't leave."

"You're the one who's leaving."

I can't believe it. I'm jogging inside the MIA. I've got to find him. Where are they? I have to catch up with them. This could be my last chance. Oh, there they are, just up ahead. Boy, I'm out of breath. Love will drive you crazy.

"Hi, Michael," I say, gasping. "I hope...um, I hope I'm not being too forward, but I'd love to invite you and Emily over for dinner. I thought maybe one night this week?"

Michael glances at Emily, and she nods. "That sounds lovely. It's a busy week, but we're available tomorrow night. Would that work?"

"Sure. Come around six. Do you like Italian food?"

"Of course. I'm Italian, you know," he says with a wink.

"Great. See you tomorrow." I watch as they disappear around another hall. I hustle back to tell Bea the great news.

"So, where did you rush off to, as if I can't guess?"

"They're coming to my place for dinner tomorrow night. Can you believe it? I've finally met my prince charming. It's going to be quite a night!"

"Cinderella, I think you've gone off your rocker."

"Don't be so negative, Bea. I think I'll make them my mom's famous spinach lasagna. And we'll drink wine like we're in Italy." Bea is giving me a weird look. "Okay, why are you staring at me like that?"

"Look, I know you're crazy about Michael, but you just met him. You know nothing about him. Slow down. Get to know him. You're sensitive to wine, maybe you should skip that part."

"Obviously, you've forgotten what it's like to be divorced, Bea. We're going to have fun, that's all. *You* had a second chance. This is *mine!*"

⁕

Take a deep breath, Donna. Inhale. Exhale. Repeat. Stop shaking, Donna, It's only six-thirty. Michael will be here any minute. He's probably stuck in traffic. Oh, God, where is he? Maybe I'll call Bea. No, she'll just tell me to chill out and relax. What if they don't show up? What if he lost my card? I think I'll pour myself a little wine.

⁕

Okay, it's seven o'clock. Something is definitely wrong. Maybe I should call 911. No, I'll have some more wine first. Yes, that will calm me down a bit. Oh, this is such great wine!

⁕

What the heck? It's seven-fifteen. I've got to call 911. I can't take this!

"911. What is your emergency?"

"Um, I, um ...Well, I'm not too sure."

"Are you in danger?"

"No, it's not that kind of emergency."

"What's going on, then?"

"Well, some friends were supposed to be here at six o'clock and they haven't arrived, and I'm wondering if maybe they got into a car accident. Is there...any way of checking?"

"I can give you the number for the Highway Patrol. You've dialed 911 which is for life-and-death emergencies. Hello? .... Are you still there? .... Hello? .... Hello?"

Oh, no! I hung up on 911. Great! Now I'm in trouble with the law. I need a tranquilizer. I wonder if I still have some left from my divorce. No, that was ten years ago. I'm sure they've expired by now.

Well, I'll just pour myself some more wine and sip it slowly. Gulp ... Gulp ... Gulp. Great wine! Gulp ... Gulp ... Gulp .... I think I'll take a short nap now.

———— ❦ ————

Holy crap! It's eight-thirty. Where the hell is he? Oh, the hell with him. I'll just finish my wine. Who needs him, anyway?"

There goes the buzzer.

"Who is it?" If it's Michael, he better have a good excuse!

"It's Michael." I buzz him in. I'm more buzzed than the buzzer. When I open the door, I see that his face is bandaged from the nose down.

"Michael, what happened to you?"

"We were in a minor car accident."

"You look terrible. Where's Emily?"

"She took a taxi home. She's fine, home resting. May I come in?"

"Of course."

I help Michael to the sofa, which isn't easy. I think I drank a little too much. I inch up to him as much as I can. He looks like a mummy with his face all bandaged. I hope he didn't ruin his perfect teeth.

"Michael, would you like a glass of wine? I could make a little hole by your mouth, and you can sip it with a straw."

"No, thanks, I'm good. An ambulance took us to the E.R. at Methodist Hospital. They said we were lucky; it could have been much worse."

"Well, thank God you're all right. I ... I thought maybe you changed your mind about me."

Michael takes my hand into his. "Donna, when you invited us to dinner, I wanted to kiss you, but Emily was right there."

"I would have let you kiss me." I take another sip of wine.

"See? That's what I love about you. You're so sexy."

"I am? No one ever said that. Not even my ex-husband!"

"Of course you are. Right now, though, I think you need to get some sleep. As soon as these bandages come off, we'll have a real date. How about dinner at your favorite restaurant, and dessert at my place?"

"Your place?" I set down my wine glass so hard it almost tips over.

"Yes, my place. We're obviously attracted to each other, Donna."

"Michael, I'm not just attracted to you. I'm in love with you."

"Donna, you're beautiful and very sexy. Let's not talk about love. Love is fleeting, love is an illusion."

Despite my efforts, I can feel tears running down my cheeks. I want love. Don't we all?

"Michael, you were married. Weren't you in love with your wife?"

"I never wanted to get married. We were young and foolish, and we married five months before Emily was born. I felt I owed her that."

"Michael, I feel a headache coming on. I've had way too much to drink."

"Donna, I'm going to be honest. I'm not interested in getting married again. I think this time in our lives is for fun and adventure, not for commitment and entanglement."

What was I thinking? I don't know Michael at all. Bea was right!

"I need time to think things through. Call me when you're feeling better and the bandages come off, okay?"

"I will, Donna." Michael gets up and goes to the door. He turns and throws me a kiss as he leaves.

———————— ⚜ ————————

"Hi, Bea. It's Donna. Can you come over tonight?"

"Sure. Are you okay?"

"Yes, I am. It's been two weeks since I heard from Michael, and I don't care. Hey, I've got some great spinach lasagna in the freezer. I'll make it tonight."

"You're not going to call him, are you?"

"No. Michael is history. Want to go back to the Mall of America this weekend? There's certainly a lot more to see."

"I'm proud of you, Donna."

<hr>

Gloria Fredkove has taken many writing classes at The Loft. In 2009 she wrote and directed a play, *Snow in the City*, which was performed by Parlor Players. Her poems have been published in *Writers in the Know* (WINK). She is a member of Women of Words (WOW) and thanks them for their encouragement, which led to two stories being published in this anthology. Gloria is writing a memoir about her childhood, *Casual Baggage*. Special thanks to husband, Joe, for his support of all of Gloria's creative endeavors, including her choral memberships in Minnesota Chorale and Singers in Accord.

The Seymore Farm for Offensive Creatures

BETTY BRANDT PASSICK

Elsa had found the half page of indecipherable hand-printed code on the Forest Heights' undergrowth outside of Hobble, Minnesota. She gazed at the paper in her hands. For the first time it occurred to her how very odd it was that Priscilla Hawkshaw and the other standing next to the car had been able to walk away to safety only seconds before the automobile exploded. Elsa recalled hearing a strange wind rustling through the trees, intermingled with a mesmerizing whisper, and wondered if perhaps Hawkshaw had heard something in the wind warning of impending danger? Right after the explosion, a red-shouldered hawk had swooped down and lopped off half of the paper in Hawkshaw's hand – the paper with the second code – and had flown off.

As for Elsa and her grey wolf, Anika, they had been miraculously saved from sure death by a black cat, which made her question whether underworld powers were at work here... *Had the cat been used unwittingly?* She knew cats were easy marks when it comes to mischief, the darker the better. But there was only one way to make a cat really do anything it would otherwise choose not to do: a caper bush. Just one whiff of the milky substance could put the minds of animals—and men—in a trance-like state long enough to get them to do most any unsavory act of another's bidding. Something had clearly gone awry if the cat was intended to guarantee anyone's demise.

The car, however, had been reduced to a steel-framed skeleton of what was a late model blue sedan. The cloth seats and rubber tires still smoldered; car pieces were scattered everywhere—a large section of the roof had flown over a dense grove of lilacs and landed a hundred feet away. Hawkshaw and the other seemed puzzled at what to do next.

Elsa, as well, found herself in a confused state of mind. Staring down at Anika at her feet, she remembered all wolves have special sensory abilities and pondered what danger the wolf had detected when trying to hold Elsa back? *Had Anika sensed the cat was somehow involved.* Anika even now growled intermittently, as though scolding the cat for its part, unwitting or not.

Elsa's mother, Anika, had psychic powers—the reason Elsa had given the wolf her mother's name. Since a young girl, Elsa knew of her mother's precognitive dreams. Most memorable was the premonition that detailed her father's death from a heart attack. Her mother saw the porch floor lined with old cardboard boxes of drying walnuts in blackened shells; her father staggering moments before his legs gave out – then, the blow to his head, cushioned by the rear wheels of Elsa's tricycle; and finally, the crow of the rooster in the chicken house at the very moment he expelled his final breath.

A second memory followed. The house where Elsa was raised had once been a barn, or so her mother said, always with a certain amount of shame. The structure was all that had been available after her parents' marriage during a particularly long season of hard economic times. Three sons and a daughter were born to the couple. Elsa's brothers had yet to display their powers, though by this time it was doubtful they'd inherited any at all—for powers are *gifts*, after all, and normally show up quite early. Thus, Elsa thought her brothers quite "ordinary."

She knew with special powers often come unpleasantries. At some point, people in Hobble began to avoid Elsa's mother. The reason may have been out of fear she may have knowledge of the impending demise of a loved one, and they simply chose not to learn of it in advance. Some even called her a "witch." For this reason, Elsa found understanding the breadth and scope of her own powers— exciting, overwhelming, and frightening, all at the same time.

Elsa refocused her attention on her faithful companion and began caressing the wolf's back of fine fur streaked with ochreous colors of yellow and orange and light gray.

"You did well in protecting us today. I can't help but wonder how you know when danger is present, and what more you might tell me if only you had the power to speak."

She saw in Anika's eyes a deep sense of loyalty, which was always of great comfort to her.

At that very second, she realized Hawkshaw must surely be anxiously awaiting her return from the woods, where she'd gone in search of the half paper dropped by the hawk. Finding the paper, she had slipped behind the narrow trunk of a Dapple Dandy Pluots tree to consider whether to return the paper to Hawkshaw. She decided to hold onto it.

At last, she and Anika emerged from the forest's edge. Sunset was underway. The sky had changed to a scattering of red, orange, and pink hues. Soon dusk would be upon them with its long, hard shadows. She could overhear Hawkshaw speaking to the other.

"While we are awaiting the police, call Joe Ritter and tell him we are in need of transportation...and tell him to deliver a pig."

"A *pig*—did I hear you right?" the other shrieked so loudly that Elsa half expected the reverberation from the echo among the towering trees to cause a sizable limb to break free and come crashing to the forest floor. *But coming so close to dying shakes everyone to their core*, she reasoned.

"Yes, a *pig*—a scrawny runt will do," Hawkshaw responded calmly. "And it needs to be...and understand this clearly...a three-legged one. I envisioned one with black diamond shapes running down its white back. Joe has such an animal at his farm. The pig has a special power, as all irregular creatures do, and will play an important role in our search to find the codes... I'll explain more later."

Suddenly, a series of clear whistled calls sliced through the skies. Elsa looked heavenward for the hawk and cowered. Anika inched closer to her side. Hawkshaw yet again concealed her piece of the half paper inside her shirt as she and the other, too, began turning in circles, looking for the bird with translucent crescents near the wingtips.

The hawk remained hidden from view, and the calls soon subsided.

Elsa and Anika continued toward Hawkshaw, who stared quizzically at her.

"I wish I had better news...that hawk has flown off with the paper. It's probably high in the nest of one of those very tall red pine trees," Elsa said.

"No worries. I think I can make out most of the code from this," Hawkshaw said, pulling the paper from her shirt and walking away, as if wanting to examine it in private.

Elsa studied Hawkshaw. *Was she truly beginning to make sense of the code?* Knowing almost nothing about Hawkshaw, she pondered how hard it would be to pry information from her.

Within a short time, Elsa thought she heard what sounded like of a high-powered V-8 engine speeding along the main gravel road leading toward them. Another fifteen minutes passed by before a dusty, late model police car with two officers pulled into the sandy, gravely clearing. The squad car came to a jarring halt, though its occupants remained inside another minute, gawking at the gutted, smoking car.

The driver was the first to emerge.

"I'm Officer Silverman and with me is Officer Havers. Someone want to tell me what's been going on out here?" he said, canvassing the area with his eyes.

Elsa observed Hawkshaw tuck the paper inside her shirt as she approached the officers.

"I'm the one who requested your presence, officer, and I wish to report an explosion," she said, pointing at the car. "Not long after our arrival this afternoon, we heard a ticking...then, BOOM! It's a miracle we all weren't killed."

"Anyone hurt? I'll need the name and address of each of you... Who wants to be first?"

Silverman proceeded to lift a flashlight from his utility belt and position it on the car's hood in such a way that the LED beam shined onto the little spiral notepad he pulled from a shirt pocket. Flipping a page, with pen in hand, he indicated he was ready to record names and statements.

Hawkshaw and the other took several steps closer to Silverman.

Elsa, too, shifted in order to remain within earshot.

Darkness was now befalling the forest with lightning speed. Havers scrambled to take photos of the remains of the vehicle and the pieces strewn about the area. Placing four-inch yellow markers next to each and measuring the distance between them, he snapped pictures with his 35mm camera with a special lens for low light. Flashes popped with such frequency that Elsa thought it was like watching the flickering lights of oversized fireflies along most any Minnesota river's edge at nightfall.

Again, she heard the calls of the hawk, this time coming from farther away. She felt relieved the bird had left the area, although Anika remained under foot, periodically growling and displaying her canine teeth whenever a breeze caused so much as a scrapping sound of a tree branch brushing up against another.

In time, Silverman asked Elsa to come forward and give her version of the incident. It took only seconds to explain how she and her pet wolf, in search of finding her *friend* Priscilla Hawkshaw, arrived on the scene just prior to the explosion. She avoided mention of any of her theories about the potential unwitting role of a cat, or of any suspected interventions of supernatural powers, or of anything else beyond the simple facts of the case. The officers seemed disinterested in Elsa as anyone qualified to explode anything.

Before the interview, Elsa thought she spotted headlights appearing and fading and reappearing in the tallest treetops near the mountain ridge. The rumble of an engine grew louder and louder as a vehicle neared. She thought everyone was aware of its imminent approach. Finally, a sleek 1950s orange Chevy pickup appeared like an apparition through a thick, dusty fog, blinding everyone within twenty-five meters of its twin headlights.

The officers, focused on finishing up their report, were caught off-guard. Startled by the intruder, almost in unison, each withdrew his holstered sidearm, pointed it in the direction of the low-down cab, and moved outside the glare of the headlights.

Elsa imagined the officers were likely thinking this was the criminal who had carried out the explosion, returning to the scene of the crime.

She repositioned herself in order to read the signage on the truck door: THE SEYMORE FARM FOR OFFENSIVE CREATURES.

Silverman barked an order at the driver: "Remain in the truck. Put your hands on the steering wheel where I can see them. State your name and business."

Havers directed his flashlight beam on the driver's face, who appeared to be a gray-bearded older gentleman wearing a boonie on his head. Small metals clipped to the cap refracted in the white light similar to falling stars in a night sky, producing glitters of silver and gold in the blackness.

A piercing squeal from the rear of the truck redirected the officers' attention.

Havers maintained the beam of his flashlight on the driver—his firearm, with the other—while Silverman slowly made his way toward the short livestock rack at the truck's rear. There, in a single bound he stepped onto the bumper and began to weave the beam of his flashlight, back to front, ultimately training the beam on one corner.

A period of silence followed before Silverman announced with equal amounts of surprise and disgust: "Believe it or not... There's a three-legged pig back here."

Havers flinched, and the flashlight beam and gun barrel in his hands drifted in tandem from the driver's face to Silverman's.

"Say that one more time," Havers said.

"I'm thinking we have a case of cruelty to animals here... What kind of a life does a pig have with only three legs? This fella should-a been put down a long time ago," he added, jumping from the bumper and marching toward the driver in a more official manner now.

Havers realigned the beam of his flashlight onto the driver, just as the old man signaled his intent to speak.

"Joe Ritter, a local, sent word to me...asking that I pick up these four – plus, he said I was to deliver a pig. You can tell by the signage on the door that I operate a farm for animals that most people wouldn't keep around any longer, it's true. But creatures with all kinds of abnormalities deserve to live full lives, just like people."

"*Who* ordered this pig?" Silverman persisted.

Hawkshaw stepped forward. "I did!" she said haltingly, as though searching for the words to explain such an oddity.

Elsa listened attentively, anxious to hear Hawkshaw's response.

Hawkshaw faced-off with Silverman, while continuing: "You see, Officers, animals of all sorts have always been of great comfort to me, and I'm especially drawn to ones who need a good home. You can imagine I'm in need of a good deal of comfort right now," pointing to the car, "for as you well know my sedan is disemboweled, eviscerated – useless! So, if you're done with your official questioning, I beg we be allowed to take leave with this man of considerable charity who has come all this way to give us a ride... including bringing with him his *adorable pig*. You can contact us at his farm with any additional questions, as may become necessary."

The officers appeared stunned by the bizarre statement.

Hearing no immediate objections, Hawkshaw and the other darted for the passenger door, opened it, climbed inside the large cab, and positioned themselves next to the driver.

Elsa took the hint, and she and Anika quickly scaled the bumper and rack—joining the three-legged pig, which quickly reverted to a corner farthest from the wolf, all the while squealing at its highest pitch. Elsa knew Anika was too tired to be menacing to a pig, and indeed, her furry friend dropped its massive body onto the steel truck bed as though preparing to sleep. After all, it had been a long, exhausting day.

Silverman, followed by Havers, retreated to the patrol car, Elsa believed, with the intent of returning to Hobble to file a police report on the loss of the sedan.

An instant later, the boonie-hatted old man turned the truck around and headed up the backroad from where it had come. Elsa sat down and stretched out her legs between the pig and Anika and breathed a sigh of relief. Their next stop would be the special farm where one and all, no matter the disability, was welcomed. Today, she had learned a little more about Hawkshaw, mostly from overhearing her responses to Officer Silverman's questioning – though she'd gleaned nothing more about deciphering the codes. She could feel the half paper pressing on her torso from inside her pocket. *Should she have come clean with Hawkshaw about finding it?* Perhaps the honesty would have gone a long way to begin to earn Hawkshaw's trust. Still, in the back of her mind, she recalled that Hawkshaw hadn't been completely honest with the officers about her intentions for the pig... *Who knew what Hawkshaw really had in mind for that animal?*

Elsa felt the air turn cool as the truck ascended the road. Resting her back and head against the side of the rack, she stared at the white pig with black diamonds down its back. Moments later, the poor thing finally grew calm enough to lie down sideways in the corner, though kept its eyes on Anika. *What special powers could a pig possibly have?* Elsa wondered. She could hardly wait to find out. A smile swathed her face at the delightful thought of what tomorrow might bring. Regardless, she had already named the beast Perspicacious, shortened to "Percy." Every creature, even a pig, deserved a home—and a name.

The truck continued making its way up the winding road in the darkness. The glow of the headlights on the trees overhead made it seem like traveling through a grand, back-lit cavern of outstretched pine-needled branches and tall, sturdy trunks. The starlite sky overhead likewise appeared as a mantle of divine protection.

Mostly, Elsa felt heartened by the fact she was in the presence of both Priscilla Hawkshaw and a three-legged pig – and that's all she really cared about. She vowed not to let them out of sight, not even for a second. Perhaps she'd yet tell Hawkshaw she'd found the half paper in the hope of getting Hawkshaw to trust her; she hadn't yet decided. Tomorrow would be a new day. But nothing was certain. Particularly, if there were underworld powers at work here.

And Elsa was sure that today wouldn't be the last time she'd see that cat.

Betty Brandt Passick is an independent author, inspirational speaker, and teacher. She has written two novels: *The Black Bag of Dr. Wiltse, Murder on the Prairie* (2021), and *Gangster in Our Midst: Bookkeeper, Lieutenant and Sometimes Hitman for Al Capone* (2017)—which won a 2019 Notable 100 Indie Book Award; plus, two memorials: *We Are Eight, a Memoriam* (2015); and *Arlington Hills Presbyterian Church, 125 Years, 1888-2013* (2014). Annually she speaks at dozens of venues, primarily in the Iowa-Minnesota-Wisconsin area. Her writing workshops include: "Writing a Memoir" (all ages), and "Journaling" (grades 5-7). Read more at www.bettybrandtpassick.com.

Truth or Fiction
KATHY ALLEN

I slowed down to a moderate speed as I whirled through the small midwestern town in Minnesota where I had grown up in the mid-1960's. I drove my high-class 1955 vintage convertible with the top down as the wind blew wildly through my long red hair. The radio blared out my favorite country music so loudly that even a hard-of-hearing person could have easily caught every lyric. I flailed my arms and my body moved fervently to the beat of the music. Over forty years had passed since I had lived in this small town, and I was on a journey back to the days of my youth and the years that I had grown up in Minnesota. The town, of course, had transformed, too, with the passage of time. I noted that the former five-and-dime store where, as a boy, I purchased candy and soda pop, had been replaced with a large, trendy department store. The barber shop where my buddies and I used to get haircuts had been replaced with a fashionable hair salon. However, I was relieved to find that the boulevards on main street were still lined with the scenic and shapely maple trees I remembered. The splendor of their fall colors was always spectacular to me, and I felt reassured that this grandeur remained the same.

The early years during which I grew up in this quaint town were not anything sensational; in fact, it was rather dull and boring. I went to school every day with my two buddies, did the usual mischief that teenage boys get into (like tossing harmless snakes at the girls), but truly nothing to brag about. My friends and I didn't even hang out with the local "sugar babes." We were more interested in playing baseball in the summer and football in the fall. We all had above average grades even though I surely do not remember that we studied a great deal. At this moment, however, I was immersed in recollections and remembrances of a time so long ago that I could not distinguish if what I remembered was actually *truth* or *fiction*.

Suddenly, out of the blue and without warning, I recalled a memory from long-ago. I was dumbfounded and did not know what to think about this sudden "blast from my past." The recollection had to do with my eighth-grade English class and a composition I had written. I was utterly stunned by this unexpected remembrance. As I continued to recall more of that decisive time and what had transpired, I did not have a good sense about the outcome of that particular event. Fortunately, I was near the local community park and immediately pulled my car over to the curb and got out. I walked slowly and reflectively to a nearby park bench and sat down. I struggled to make sense of what my mind had just dredged up. My heart beat profusely, and I began to sweat. I did not have much recollection of my past since experiencing a severe head trauma fifteen years ago. Memories of important milestones, key events, and significant people of my past life had not returned; that is, up until now. Although I admit, in recent months, a few of these remembrances had begun flooding back. Little by little, these small recollections had given me the expectation and anticipation that I would one day have total memory recall, and that belief provided me with a degree of confidence and hope.

As I sat on the park bench, thoughtful and meditative, I struggled to compose myself. I took several deep breaths and closed my eyes. As I slowly began to relax, my eyelids became very heavy, and I fell into a deep sleep. Suddenly I woke up. I was confused and at first did not remember where I was. After a number of minutes had passed, I grasped that I had had the most amazing, true-to-life dream about the events that occurred in my English class so many, many years ago. The longer I sat on that bench, the more I recalled a great deal of what had occurred. I thought to myself, "*A dream or reality; fabrication or actuality?*"

I now vividly remembered that I had decided to finish the written composition assignment and that I had turned it in to my English teacher. The story, in fact, sounded quite improbable and so far-fetched that no one would believe a fabrication like this one. Most of us have heard of a student's excuse to their teacher for not having their homework assignment completed and one of them is: "my dog ate my homework." So then, my reader, maybe it is not my total imagination. I will let you decide for yourself. Read on.

I walked slowly to the front of the classroom and, with a stern look and hands on her hips, my English teacher fixed her eyes on both me and on the covered, white ice-cream bucket that I held in my quivering hands. She scrutinized me and then she scrutinized the bucket. Finally, after what seemed like an eternity and with a tone in her voice that I did not particularly like, she asked, "Young man, what is in that bucket you are holding?"

"Well, Ma'am," I answered awkwardly, "It's my homework assignment. And I was to turn it in today, remember?"

"Of course, I remember," she retorted with irritation. "I'm the teacher who gave you the assignment, but what is it doing in that disgusting-looking bucket? From what I can see, the contents do not look very appealing, and now it seems to be releasing an aroma that is definitely not agreeable. I would like an explanation from you, and I would like it without further disruption," she stated emphatically.

"All right," I answered timidly.

As I slowly removed the cover and looked inside, the contents did not look anything like they did the night before. My teacher was right, the contents did not look appealing, and they were beginning to emit a foul odor that indeed was not agreeable.

How could that be? I thought to myself. When I went to bed last night, the contents looked fairly presentable as homework, not perfect by any means, but to some degree presentable. How would I explain this to my teacher? She may have a hard time believing this was my homework assignment. But I hoped that she would know that I was telling the truth after I enlightened her with what had occurred the night before.

I was brought back to the present-day when my teacher asked again with frustration, "Let me have a look inside of that bucket." I slowly moved away and let her take a look inside. The response from her was not at all what I expected. "Oh, my," she gasped and turned a pasty white. "What is that disgusting-looking white material in there and, oh my, that smell is without question repulsive."

"Please, I can explain," I answered back. "Or at least I think I can explain," as I tried to sound credible. I cringed and realized she would never believe what happened last night and how that nauseating mess in the bucket was supposed to be my homework. I wondered if I should go ahead with what in fact happened and or do I just give up and let her think that I did not do my homework assignment? An incomplete would be better than this torment that I have endured, but instead I said respectfully to my teacher, "Okay. This is what took place, and it is the truth. My dog ate my homework."

⚜

As my teacher scowled at me and waited for me to further explain the situation, I worried that she'd never believe this story that my dog ate my assignment. Would I believe a story like that? No, I most likely would not. It would just be an excuse someone fabricated for not doing what they are supposed to do, like a homework assignment. At last, with clammy palms, I proceeded to tell what transpired the night before.

It was well past my bedtime when I finally completed the assignment. I had placed it in a folder and laid it on top of my desk. Because I was so tired and wanted to get into bed, I did not take extra precautions to put my assignment inside my top desk drawer where it would be safe from any intruder. The family dog had an unpleasant habit in that whatever was laid down, he claimed for himself and would proceed to chew it to shreds or eat it. Unfortunately for me, this night I had forgotten to put my important homework assignment inside the safety of the desk drawer. A not so forgiving blunder that I would soon discover.

I paused and looked at my teacher anxiously. She nodded her head which I understood to mean, "Resume with your senseless narrative."

So, I continued. I stated that at about 3:00 a.m., I was awakened to a dreadful sound of retching and gagging coming from the center of my bedroom. It was totally dark, but I recognized that sound and knew that it was definitely coming from the dog. Because I was so tired, I did not want at all to deal with whatever the dog had gotten into. I would take care of it in the morning. I turned over in my bed to go back to sleep when a gnawing feeling came over me. I thought to myself: *there really is nothing in my bedroom the dog could get into, is there?* Didn't I put everything away? With a panic that made my own stomach want to retch, I jumped out of my bed and turned on the lamp.

———————— ❧ ————————

What I saw in the middle of the room made me wish that I had not turned on the light, and that I had stayed in bed for the remainder of the night. I was ready to completely forget about turning in my assignment and take an incomplete. It was a nightmare, yes, it had to be. First, I looked over at my desk, then I looked at our pet dog, who sat in the middle of the room, and then I looked at what was on the floor. My homework was not on my desk but instead, to my overwhelming misfortune, it lay in a pile on the floor, tattered and in shreds, where my dog had retched it up. I went over and examined the remains. It was a jumbled mess but by a quirk of fate I still could see the writing and it was legible. It was legible! I could not believe my luck. All I had to do was piece back together the shredded remains and turn in my assignment tomorrow morning as planned. A great but not a well-thought-out plan. It would, without a doubt, be an unpleasant task and I would be up the remainder of the night trying to patch up what the dog had eaten, but at that particular moment I was not worried. All I wanted to do was piece together what was left of my tattered homework.

I labored most of that night taping together the unpleasant retched-up fragments of my homework and placed each squishy piece of paper carefully into an old ice cream bucket that I found in my closet. At last, my work was completed, and if I did say so myself, the homework looked passable enough to turn in to my English teacher. I only hoped that the smell would quickly dissipate. I placed a lid on the bucket, tumbled into my bed and fell into a deep, but shortened, sleep.

I awoke abruptly to the sound of the alarm that had been going on and off for quite some time. Not surprisingly, I had managed to oversleep. I threw back the covers and leapt out of my bed. I hurriedly brushed my teeth, put on fairly clean clothes, picked up the bucket, and ran down the stairs to hastily eat my breakfast. I then grabbed my school bag and the bucket with the retched-up, patched-up schoolwork, and ran out to meet the school bus, which I almost missed (in some way, I suppose that in all honesty, I secretly wanted to miss that bus).

Everyone on the bus wondered what was in the bucket that I held warily in my hand and snickered when I said, "It's my homework assignment." They snickered again because they could see and smell that there was something rather strange looking in the bucket.

I waited until all of the students got off the bus before I walked to the front. I was about to get off when the bus driver just had to make a one final snide comment. "Hey, sonny, whatcha got in that there bucket? It does not smell all that great," he snickered. "It's my homework," I answered, annoyed and irritated. I swiftly made my exit.

I walked slowly because my shoes felt heavy, like they had cement in them. I thought to myself, *My homework is a mess because of my dog.* Would my English teacher believe me? I certainly planned to tell the truth even if my teacher found it hard to believe. I reasoned this has to be an outlandish dream or a practical joke that I will soon awaken from. I headed through the revolving school door, walked to the English classroom and sat down in my desk and waited. And waited. Heart pounding.

I stood before my teacher, head bowed low, looking at my dirty tennis shoes. I should have worn cleaner shoes today. The anxiety I felt was beyond words. I knew the account that I told my teacher was true. That my pet dog truly did eat my homework and threw it up all over the floor. I worked hard to put those papers back together, but it just did not work out. After what seemed like forever, I lifted my head and looked directly into her eyes.

Just as I expected to hear my teacher pronounce her verdict of *truth* or *fiction,* out of the blue and without warning, my mind screamed, *Oh, no, what just happened?* I was sitting on that park bench, and could not believe that I no longer had the memories from a few moments ago?" Whatever I had recalled had utterly and completely vanished. Gone, departed, no more, wiped out. I knew for certain that only a second ago I was on the brink of a breakthrough. A breakthrough where I was about to remember what had taken place in that eighth-grade English classroom. The beginning of the memory had been very vivid, but now it was scattered and missing from my mind.

I struggled to summon up what the assignment had been about. Did I completely fabricate the story I had just experienced? For the life of me, I could not conjure up any recollections about the details. How could the recollections just cease to exist? They had vanished and were nowhere to be found. I was confused and my mind could not comprehend what just transpired. I came to the conclusion that I no longer wished to dwell on these past events, and so I slid myself back into my 1955 vintage convertible and drove out of that small Minnesota town at a moderate speed, top down, wind blowing wildly through my long red hair. This time, however, I did not have the radio turned on to my favorite country music. I mused to myself, "Will I never remember the events of my past? And, if and when I do, what are the odds of them staying with me? Suddenly a sheet of paper landed on my windshield and rested where it hindered my field of vision. So, I slowly pulled over to the side of the road where I could safely lift off the paper. Once in my hands, I was curious to read what it said. Imagine my astonishment when I read the following words: "Eighth Grade Writing Assignment: My Dog Ate My Homework." Written by … Much to my disappointment, the signature was not decipherable. The paper I held in my hand clearly had gotten wet and was moldy and dirty. The title on the paper seemed vaguely familiar. I turned it over in my hands a couple of times for any recognition and when I realized that it did not mean anything to me, I tossed the paper along the road side, got back into my car and continued on. "What was that all about anyway?" I thought to myself, confused. As the saying goes, "Truth can be stranger than fiction." What do you, readers, think about this tale? *Truth or fiction?*

 The tragic death of Kathy's son, Bryon, is what inspired her to write about her journey of grief and ultimate healing of her broken heart. She wants to bring comfort to those in sorrow and heartache just as God has brought comfort to her.

When Kathy is not writing, she enjoys spending time with her family, friends and, unquestionably, with her ten grandchildren. In the summertime, she enjoys gardening and, in the winter, she and her husband, Roger, enjoy the warm sunshine of the Rio Grande Valley in Texas. She and Roger have been married for over 50 years and they reside in Minnesota where they live in a small retirement community.

Welcome Home

Ann Aubitz

———— ⚜ ————

As I shuffled across the carpet in my giant pink bunny slippers, I was ambushed by negative thoughts, stopping me from enjoying my first day off in months. It was a terrible time to have these thoughts. My new album would be dropping tomorrow, and my world tour started in a few weeks. Today was supposed to be the beginning of a relaxing four-week vacation—the vacation where I thought I would be getting engaged on our one-year anniversary. I should have been enjoying my time off, not moping around my cabin watching the same video clip on repeat.

As soon as the clip first aired on television, I had jumped on a plane to northern Minnesota, which I call home. Even during the winter, the sound of the wind whistling through the treetops relaxes me like nothing else. The crisp air and beautiful pristine white landscape beckon me home. Of course, the activities during the summer are even more incredible: water skiing, hiking, swimming—you name it. I always laughed at my friends from California who assumed that Minnesota was cold year-round.

With a dramatic thump, I sat down, draped my legs over the arm of my favorite comfy chair, picked up the remote, and changed the channel, only to see the same video playing again. My boyfriend, or should I say, my new ex, had unceremoniously dumped me on a trashy late-night talk show, telling the world Ava Myers was a great girl...but not marriage material because she had a deep dark secret. He didn't seem to think this when he was a struggling actor, and I was a "mega-hit music superstar"—at least that's what the tabloids called me. I got him his first and only role in a big-budget movie, and this is how he repaid me.

"Ugh," I groaned out loud, turning down the volume. This was my least favorite part of the interview.

"She acts so refined and so...sssophishticated—but she's not," my ex blurted out after the host simply asked him how I was doing.

"What do you mean *acts*?" the bewildered host replied. "Ava is talented and successful. She's always so nice to everyone. I think she's amazing."

"Here's...da thing. Iss all just an act," he said, slurring his words. "Iss not who she really is. She has a secret."

My ex, Sam, was all looks and no substance. He was breathtakingly handsome, almost too pretty, with his perfect blond hair and big green eyes. He was a model-turned-actor who was cast in one of my music videos about a year ago. The rest, they say, is history.

Photos flashed up on the screen behind them. There I was, with my blonde hair and blue eyes, posing with every guy I have ever worked with within the last ten years. The suggestion was clear: these men were my many conquests. What nonsense! I did not date all those men. Sadly, I could count the number of men I have been involved with on one hand.

"See, why da you think she goes out with sooo many men? She's…not the marrying type." He hiccupped, then struggled with his words again. "Iss what I'm tryin' ta tell you. She's not at all what…she seems."

In a way, he was right. Lately, I had felt less like a mega-hit superstar and more like a fraud. When I'd started in the music business ten years ago, I'd dreamed of becoming what I am today: a famous award-winning pop star. For some reason, I didn't think I would have to give up so much to do it. I felt like I lost myself in the process of becoming famous.

When I met my manager, I was a sixteen-year-old girl who had moved from a small town in northern Minnesota to Hollywood to make it big. All I had was my guitar, my voice, and forty bucks in my pocket. I had to listen to my manager then. I didn't know any better. But now… *Get a grip, Ava. You've made your decisions, and you must live with them. You've been luckier than most. Stop whining.*

My thoughts were interrupted by the buzzing of my phone. I looked at the screen. Finally, someone was calling who I actually wanted to talk to.

"Hello, Eddie."

"Hi Ava, still moping around?"

"Why would you think I'm moping?"

"Because I know you. I bet you've watched the video clip a hundred times already. So, stop torturing yourself and go out with me—right now."

"I don't think I would be very good company. And aren't you in the cities?" I sat upright in my chair and looked down at my bunny slippers.

"I'm right outside your door. Stop wallowing in self-pity and get ready for a big day. Bring along sunglasses, sunscreen, and a hat."

"I can't."

"Yes, you can. I happen to know you have nothing scheduled for the next four weeks because you had a vacation planned with your loser ex-boyfriend. So now you're spending your vacation with me. Get out of your pajamas, take off your bunny slippers, and get in the truck."

"How did you know I was still in my pajamas?" I wondered if I was becoming too predictable.

"Because I know you, Ava. You constantly waste your time with the wrong guys, then you live like a hermit in your PJs and torment yourself. He was never good enough for you, and you know it. Now get ready!"

"Okay, you win. I could use a diversion. Give me twenty minutes."

"You have ten. Move it, girl," Eddie said with his cool ease.

"Yes, sir."

———————— ❧ ————————

After ten minutes there was a loud knock at the door. My time was up. I flung the door open and on the other side was my best friend, Eddie. The gap-toothed, small-town boy I grew up with didn't look like a little boy anymore. The last ten years of only seeing his face on our infrequent video calls didn't do him justice. Little Eddie had filled out. His face was less boyish than I remembered, and his features were chiseled. His brown hair was cut short for the sweltering summer months in Minnesota, but he left just a touch of dark scruff on his face that gave him a roguish look. Paired with his dark eyes, I was intrigued by this man standing in front of me and a little sad that I'd missed his transition from the little boy I loved.

"Ava, it is so good to see you. I've missed you!" He grabbed me and held me in a big bear hug for a little longer than the friendly hugs I remembered from him. My heart rate increased, and my body tingled at his touch. I had to remind myself this was my best friend, Eddie.

In the truck on the way to I don't know where, I sighed as I glanced at the article on my phone one more time. The reporter went into detail about my rocky past, lack of parental guidance, and fleeting relationships with men. The thing was, I didn't have a rocky past, or any of that other stuff. I had a very nice, normal, midwestern upbringing. My manager, Barnaby, concocted the story about my past because he thought I would garner more sympathy and attention if people thought I was a troubled youth from small-town Minnesota making it big in LA. What a crock. He never truly believed in my talent; he just wanted to make me into his next cookie-cutter pop star.

Returning the phone to my purse, I looked out the window and watched the beautiful landscape streaking by.

"I forgot how beautiful it is here. Where are we going?"

"I'm not going to tell you until we're there, but you'll probably guess before then. I am so happy you are home; it has been too long." Eddie looked so sad when he said this, and suddenly the decision I made all those years ago felt wrong. "I hope you'll spend all your time off with me and decide if you want to see your family. I know they would love to see you."

"Yeah, I know."

"Sorry for bringing it up. I know you have some things to work out with your folks, and I know you thought Sam was going to propose to you on your one-year anniversary. But Ava—seriously, you dodged a bullet with that guy."

Eddie had it wrong, I wasn't sad about Sam; I was sad about missing the years with Eddie. I wasn't sure what to say so I concentrated on the view out my window. My breath caught in my throat as we sped down the freeway on the way to the cities. The beauty of the fall colors was just peeking out on this amazingly hot early September day. I looked up and saw literally my favorite place in the whole world: the Minnesota State Fair. The bridge over the street was crammed with people all excited to make it through the main gates.

"Wow," I whispered.

"I know, it's so nostalgic. I remember all the times we were here as kids."

"Why is it that we haven't come back here?"

"Ava, you moved away when you were sixteen and haven't come home recently. You've been dating Sam for the last year, you were busy recording your new album, and you haven't had any time for me."

"You know it's not true, and I always have time for you. I'm sorry if it felt like that while I was gone."

"I missed you, Ava." He smiled and looked into my eyes. For a moment I thought he was going to kiss me. Then he moved away and concentrated on the long line of cars leading into the parking area.

I looked over at Eddie and instantly felt a pain in my heart for hurting him. I didn't realize I'd neglected him when I left for LA and, more recently, while I went out with Sam. I remember the good times with Eddie. Our families lived next to each other north of the Twin Cities in an extremely small town. Eddie and I were practically raised as brother and sister. We saw each other every day. He would come over for camp outs and sleep overs with me and my sister. We had such a great time hiking through the woods, burning our marshmallows for smores, and catching fireflies in jars, then poking holes in the lid. All the stuff that kids did growing up in northern Minnesota. I hadn't realized until now how much I missed it. I'd buried myself in work all these years to fill the hole I was feeling for not having my family or Eddie with me.

I was used to traveling with a bodyguard, personal assistant, and my manager, but this time, I'd left without telling them where I was going. There would be hell to pay tomorrow, I was sure, but today, I was free. Or maybe not—my phone was blowing up with messages. There were fifteen from my manager Barnaby, so I thought I better call him before we went into the fair so I could enjoy my day without the anxiety of my phone buzzing in my purse.

"I'm sorry Eddie; I have to make a phone call before we go in."

"Can't it wait until tomorrow?"

"No, if I don't call my manager back, he'll just keep calling, and calling, and calling." I held up my phone to show the fifteen missed calls. "I'll feel better if I get this over with so we can enjoy the day."

"I understand. Go ahead, but I don't think he is the right manager for you if he doesn't understand you." Eddie wiggled the truck into the space the orange-vested teen was waving us into.

"Hello Barnaby."

"Hello? Is that all I get?" He sounded infuriated, which was his normal mood with me lately.

"It is the polite thing to say when you call someone. What do you need Barnaby?"

"I need you to come home, right now."

"I am home Barnaby. I am at my cabin in Minnesota. Everything is fine and can wait until I return."

"No Ava, everything is not fine. Your image is not fine. First, Sam goes on national television and tells everyone you have a secret. Now people are digging to find out what your secret is. Guess what? You do have a secret. You've been lying to your fans for all these years. Second, you leave this mess and go to a different state to hide out."

There was a pause. I decided this was a good time to let Eddie hear the whole conversation and I hit the speaker button and motioned to him to start recording it.

I had to stand up to Barnaby once and for all. Eddie was right. Barnaby wasn't the right manager for me—not then, not now. "Barnaby, I did *not* make the lie up about my family. You did. And I am *not* coming back to LA. I'm going to hang out with my family. I won't be back for at least four weeks, maybe longer."

Barnaby didn't let me finish my sentence. "You're coming home today!" He was seething and breathing hard into the phone. "I'll have a private jet standing by at the Minneapolis airport. If you know what's good for you, you'll come home without another word." As he said this, I found myself shaking, not with fear, but with anger.

"That sounds like a threat. That's it, Barnaby, we're done. You're fired!"

"You can't fire me! I have a contract."

"With what you just said to me and what I have documented from our past, you are in violation of the morals clause in your contract. Goodbye Barnaby."

All I heard was some incoherent stammering from Barnaby, then I disconnected the call.

"Wow Ava, I am so proud of you. You're amazing."

"Thank you, Eddie, but it was a long time coming. I shouldn't have let him bully me into lying about my family and my past. Now let's go get some cheese curds."

"Sounds good to me."

We got out of the car and started the walk across the grassy parking area. Walking up the ramp, on the bridge that stretched over the street, always signified to me that a day of fun was about to ensue. I still had that excited feeling in the pit of my stomach—that happy feeling not only from the fair, but from being with Eddie.

I had fond memories of going to the fair with Eddie and our families. We would pile into the car at a ridiculously early time in the morning and get to the fair just as it opened and start at Machinery Hill, where all the big farm equipment was located. We would sit on all the tractors pretending we were driving them around our farmland. After the machines, we would head to the barns, and I would sing to all the chickens, pigs, and cows that would listen. This is where I got my practice singing to large groups. The next stop was the dairy building and watching the butter carver carve images of the dairy princesses into large slabs of butter. Once she was done, they would take the butter shavings and put them on saltine crackers and pass them out to the crowd. When I'm feeling homesick, I get the saltines and butter out and have a special snack.

"Should we do our same fair route, or would you like to start with the barns since they're closest?" Eddie asked.

"I would love to start with the barns."

Eddie grabbed my hand as we walked around cow patties that littered the street. Once we were clear of the obstacles, I was sure he would drop my hand, but he held onto it as we walked up the concrete walkway to the barn. He turned to look at me as we walked through the doors and gave me such a tender look I felt like crying.

I can't believe I didn't see this before. All those years wasted because I had to chase a dream—a dream that I didn't even seem to want as much as my manager did.

"Well, here we are Ava, among your fans."

I didn't even think about it. I just started singing as soon as we were by the stalls. The cows looked up from their lunch as I belted out a song from my last album. Too late, I realized I probably shouldn't have started singing in front of the humans.

People turned and stared as it dawned on them who I was. I had forgotten that I usually travel with an entourage and now it was just me and Eddie.

He didn't even hesitate. He grabbed my hand and pulled me through the back door into the alley.

"Oh, Eddie I am so sorry. I totally forgot that people would recognize me if sang. Now I've ruined our beautiful day."

"Ava, you haven't ruined anything." He said as he lightly touched my face and stepped closer. I could feel his breath on my cheek. His lips lightly touched mine, and he backed a way for a moment to make sure that I was okay, then gave me a deep, passionate kiss—one I never thought I would get from my best friend. I realized then that even though I'd been gone for years, the relationship I shared with Eddie was timeless and I was never leaving him again.

He stepped back and whispered, "Welcome home, Ava."

Ann Aubitz is the Co-owner and Publisher of Kirk House Publishers and FuzionPress, located in Burnsville, Minnesota. After years of reading everything she could get her hands on, she decided to help others achieve their dream of becoming an author. Her mission is to help authors reach their objectives by seeing their books in print.

Ann is also a proud member of the Independent Book Publishers Association, a Board Member-At-Large for the Midwest Independent Publishers Association, and a group leader for Women of Words and chairs the yearly WOW writing conference. Kirkhousepublishers.com

When Everything Changed

ALANA FAULK

Autumn stood, waiting impatiently outside the glass doors of the Delta arrival gate. Her hand shook just a bit as she slid the last Marlboro Light out of the pack. As she fumbled through her sweatshirt pocket, searching hastily for a lighter, she was reminded of the promise she had made to herself to quit smoking. She had, in fact, stopped for almost six months but the events of the day had triggered a relapse. *Well, this is really* it—*the final smoke, the last cigarette of my life,* she vowed as she lit the tip of her Marlboro and inhaled deeply. Autumn strode along the sidewalk until she reached an aluminum bench next to the red brick building. Tired of standing, she plopped down onto the chilly seat and her mind drifted back to an icy cold January evening and a conversation which had occurred in her little, one-bedroom Colorado apartment.

"Tell me you aren't really thinking of keeping it!" he had shouted at her, the confrontation sounding more like a threat than a question. Those appalling words had sent a chill through her veins and bounced around inside of her head for weeks after he'd unleashed them. Staring into his cold, hard eyes, she could not find a single trace of the man she'd fallen in love with nearly two years before.

Upon meeting, there had been an intense physical attraction between them. Randy, drawn first to her unpretentious, subtle beauty, later found her brazen tongue and cheeky attitude alluring in a curious, inexplicable way. Autumn, on the other hand, had so enjoyed the cat-and-mouse game she skillfully played with this dark and handsome stranger, even though it had been love at first sight on her part. Playing hard to get became exceedingly difficult for the young lovers as their physical attraction for one another turned to passionate desire. They became intimate, inseparable, and undividable. Friends and family frowned upon their youthfulness and the intensity of their romance, telling them to slow down. Tired of the scrutiny and looking for adventure, there came a day when they hatched a plan to move out west. Colorado seemed a pleasant destination. Minnesota had become boring, monotonous, and dreary. Craving excitement and freedom, the pair rented a U-Haul that spring, packed it up, and gleefully said goodbye to everything and everyone they had ever known.

Initially, the excitement of the adventure was intoxicating. On this journey, they had discovered a newfound freedom they had never been afforded and with that liberty came the ability to make their own choices, some of which happened to be very poor decisions. They found an apartment on the seedy side of town where they discovered a new collection of cronies and cohorts who enjoyed a good time more than a quiet life. The group of very young adults partied hard and heavy which made keeping a job a difficult task. Autumn had found and lost four jobs in just as many months. Randy worked on and off for a bit, in fact, just enough to keep the lights on and the landlord off his back. Eventually, the good times turned to difficult times. Their lack of money fueled a fire of discontent, and their laid-back, easygoing relationship began to crumble.

Autumn savored the last drag of her final cigarette and sighed as she blew out the smoke and dropped the butt onto the sidewalk beneath her feet. She flattened the glowing embers as she stood up to head inside. Looking at her watch, it was 7 p.m. The plane was due to arrive shortly, and her nerves would no longer tolerate the stillness of sitting motionless on the bench. She strolled into the terminal to warm up and once again, wait. As she walked aimlessly through the building, her thoughts began to wander again as she recalled her visit to the cold, sterile room she'd been seated in at the Denver free clinic.

"Congratulations," the doctor had said with an apprehensive smile, "you're going to have a boy...a strong, healthy boy." Autumn's heart had stopped, and she had felt as though she might faint right there in the office. She had felt so conflicted at the time. Her heart raced with unmitigated, eager excitement while her mind flooded itself with nervous apprehension. She'd done it this time. There would be no way to talk her way out of this mess.

As the weight began to settle on her once petite frame, and the morning sickness replaced the pre-baby hangovers, Autumn knew she could no longer hide this ruinous secret from Randy. This predicament would not just go away. She began to wonder if the news of this baby—*his* baby—might bring them closer. Perhaps he would be overjoyed or at least happy at the thought of having a son? She had decided to share the news that afternoon, and predictably, Randy was far from overjoyed.

He sat there on the sofa, breathing heavy, arms crossed, staring at her as if she were Satan. He huffed and sighed and slammed his head onto the back of the couch, squeezing his eyes closed. There were no hugs or smiles, and the room began to feel suffocating with gloom and despair. Autumn could say, with definite certainty, she had indeed reached the lowest point of her life at that very moment. Her world came crashing down as Randy's next comment spewed from his mouth. "What are you thinking? My God, we can barely feed ourselves!" he shouted as he stood up and stormed out of the tiny apartment, slamming the door behind him. For a moment, she wondered if maybe Randy was right. She had no idea how to raise a baby. Perhaps she should get rid of the baby, or at least give it to someone who could afford to take care of it.

Autumn felt the tears well up and finally burst from her eyes. She sat there, alone in the apartment, and continued to cry as the afternoon sun dropped from the sky. She fell asleep on the couch, waiting for Randy to return. She awoke to sunshine in her eyes and a silent, empty apartment. Autumn realized she needed her family and friends, and it was time to go home. She reached for the phone and dialed her mother's number. They talked for hours, and that afternoon, she found herself soaring across the sky back to Minnesota. That was then.

The loudspeaker lit up the room with the announcement that Delta flight 377 from Denver had landed, abruptly jerking Autumn back to the present moment. Her heart beat wildly as her eyes searched the terminal for his face, even though, in all reality, he could not have even gotten off the plane yet. She began to speculate if maybe she should have brought the baby in with her for this little family reunion. She had considered it but had decided the airport was not where she wanted father and son to meet. David, or little DJ for short, was outside waiting in the car with his grandmother. She had only contemplated bringing him in because Randy had missed so much already. Autumn had elected to remain in Minnesota with her family and have the baby there. Finding herself away from judgmental eyes and negative accusations, it became clear to her that although she was petrified beyond belief, she could never, *ever* give up this baby. They had stayed in contact through the pregnancy, attempting graciously to work their issues out, but things were different now. Something had changed. Well, no, *everything* had changed, including Autumn.

The passengers began filing through the gate as she waited with anxious anticipation. They flowed into the terminal in a steady wave of people, but Randy was nowhere to be seen. Autumn's head began to swim as the wave turned into a trickle and eventually, no one else came through the gate. And still she waited, hoping he would come running to her, smiling that unforgettable smile she had fallen in love with, and cover her face with kisses...dozens of loving kisses. She stood there in sad disbelief and her knees grew weak. She sat down on the floor, cross-legged, in the middle of the empty waiting area. She thought at first that she might begin to cry, but the tears did not come. Instead, she felt strength inside like she had never felt before. Feeling silly sitting there, she pulled herself to her feet and marched out the door to her mother's waiting car.

As she approached the vehicle and saw her mother's concerned face, she wished in vain she had saved one last cigarette. But that craving disappeared as soon as she saw her little DJ strapped in his car seat. Autumn opened the back door and lifted him out of the seat, feeling an overwhelming sensation of emotion fill her heart. She hugged him to her chest and smelled the delicate, musky smell of his hair and now, the tears did fall. She was suddenly overwhelmed by the infinite amount of love she felt for this tiny human being. This innocent child, who looked up at her with eyes identical to her own and a hint of his daddy's irresistible smile, and she knew *this* little man would love her forever. She realized, regrettably, that she had taken too many foolish risks in her life and made so many mistakes and bad choices, but this pure and beautiful child was not one of them. Randy would not be around to watch this incredible baby grow and thrive, but she would be there, always. No, she did not need Randy anymore, for she had fallen in love with another boy...a charming, handsome, twelve-pound boy.

Alana Marie is a Minnesota author, whose tales and yarns are based on actual events that have occurred throughout her very colorful life. Some of the stories may revolve around the trials and tribulations of friends and family but all include some shred of truth. Alana, herself, is an out and proud lesbian who once weighed 528 pounds. A former bar and nightclub owner with a serious infatuation for food and alcohol, she has overcome tremendous obstacles throughout the years. Now sober for more than a decade, she has published two books on Amazon under *the Pick a Struggle Cupcake* title. Alana has also been published in *Chicken Soup for the Soul* and *WW Thin-line magazine*. In sharing experiences and recovery in a raw, yet sensitive fashion, she hopes to inspire, provoke and motivate others to take the steps necessary to chase their dreams and conquer their own demons and dilemmas. Enjoy her stories and struggles...they come from the heart.

The Widows of Woodhill

Kathi Holmes

——— ❧ ———

Continuously, all day, the garage door at the Woodhill Condominiums opens and closes. One by one the widows head out as if the gate had been left open in the stable and the horses galloped their way out into the world. Some are headed for the healthy foods' grocery store—the one their husbands thought was far too expensive. Others are meeting girlfriends for an early lunch. A routine far too long neglected. These are the survivors. They have won the longevity battle and are ready to reap the rewards.

The years turned into decades; the decades surpassed the half-century mark. The marriages survived. The children were grown. The grandchildren were having children. Through often tumultuous events, the marriages survived. Often, deteriorating health scares generated ambulance calls, hospital visits and stays at transitional care centers. Walkers plodded the halls. Knees were replaced. Hearts were mended. The marriages survived. Then, the final call came. One by one they became widows.

Most did not move into Woodhill with the thought of becoming a widow. Far from it. They were merely downsizing from the larger family homes they both no longer wanted to maintain, living out their "golden years" traveling, entertaining and socializing.

Although some of the women had become widows at a younger age, most of the women were older. Woodhill was not officially a senior community; however all the current residents were over 65.

Today the obit section of the paper announced a new member would join the Widows of Woodhill. There was a funeral to plan, condolences to be received and a new life to be embarked on.

Over half the 24 units were occupied by widows. These women were single, but they didn't lack a social life. Day in and day out they were on the move. Like ants scurrying to a picnic.

Their comeback started with reigniting social circles. Getting back into Bridge clubs, Mahjong games, book clubs or fitness centers. Then there was planning for winter escapes or long-awaited trips to faraway places. Some reinvented themselves and sunk their souls into a dream job. One of the widows found an array of interesting people when she began helping her daughter run her elder hostel. Another spent her days nurturing her interior design business, while yet another found comfort in retrieving her former career and became a volunteer teacher three days a week.

Whatever their choice, all the women found time for a weekly trip to the beauty shop and regularly scheduled manicures and pedicures. The mantra they were raised with: a woman should always look her best.

Late afternoon cars lined up with friends waiting to pick them up for dinner at a new restaurant, the opening night of a new stage production, the latest movie release, an operatic chestnut or a Mozart concert.

A few widows found widowers with which to share their experiences. Although the company of a man was welcome, there was never a need to seal the deal or even to combine residences. The widows had flexibility and freedom, and they liked it that way.

Their days were busy and full. It was only after they arrived home for the evening or in the early morning before they got started that they felt emptiness. This was a small price to pay for the hustle and bustle of a life well lived.

Then it happened. The first widower moved into Woodhill. He was shy, reserved and appeared to be in good health. He was noticed. It wasn't long before he was the subject of chatter among the widows.

"Did you know his wife died two years ago?"

"He doesn't seem to have any children visiting him."

"He moved here from Chicago."

The curiosity continued, each contributing a little more to his story.

Paul had a lengthy career as an engineer in Chicago. He planned that he and his wife, Ann, would enjoy spending more time at the cabin on the lake and possibly traveling to exotic places.

However, that didn't happen. When Ann had a debilitating stroke, they moved to Minnesota to move closer to her family. They sold their house in a Chicago suburb, packed up only what they needed and rented a home in south Minneapolis near her sister and her family.

Being retired, Paul was able to spend the last two years as a full-time caregiver for his wife. He had had a responsible career, yet he found caregiving much harder than he thought. Between cooking meals, arranging doctor and physical therapy appointments, and grocery shopping, he was unable to leave her, so he never had a chance to get to know the Twin Cities. His sister-in-law and her family were not a lot of help because they had their own family to care for. After his wife died, the rented house was too big for him, so he moved to Woodhill, a condo in the first ring suburbs of Minneapolis. Paul didn't realize when he signed the deed that he was the only widower in the building.

Paul wasn't what you would call handsome, but he was always clean shaven and had a very calm, pleasant demeanor. His smile seemed to sneak up on him and made his blue eyes shine. When he smiled you hardly noticed he was slightly overweight. When passing him in the hall, he left a faint whiff of a woodsy scent behind. He was noticed.

The ladies were eager to welcome Paul.

Evelyn was a small petite lady with a vibrant personality. She had the unit adjacent to Paul. At 89, Evelyn still managed to organize most of the parties within the condominium, so she couldn't resist having an introductory party for Paul. The ladies swarmed in to learn more about this young, but not too young, man. They sipped wine, laughed and even joked about Paul being the only man they let in the condo.

Evelyn was frisky and took a daily walk, except when the Minnesota winters prevented it. In the summer she drove around town in her sky-blue vintage Austin-Healey with the top down. That was her baby, and she spent an exorbitant amount of money getting it tuned up each spring.

When Evelyn heard Paul hadn't seen most of the sights of her great city, she decided to take him under her wing and introduce him to the Twin Cities. She was excited to show Paul the sites in her little sports car. Men do like cars.

It was a gorgeous summer day. What Minnesotans call a "Number 10" day. They meandered around Lake Calhoun, winding onto the road around Lake Harriet.

"That's the bandshell where they have music concerts all summer long," Evelyn said, imagining listening to the sweet sounds of music sitting next to Paul.

The sun was sparkling like diamonds on the water and Evelyn's short grey hair was fluffing in the wind. She had a nice-looking "young" man seated next to her on this picturesque day. Life was good.

"Oh, you've just got to see the famous Spoonbridge and Cherry sculpture in the Minneapolis Sculpture Garden." He had seen pictures of it but never up close. They wandered around looking at all the sculptures.

"Why is that rooster blue?"

"It was inspired by a sculpture in London. The rooster represents a symbol of France, painted in a French blue and it celebrated a major victory in the Napoleonic wars. To us, it just gives visitors something to wonder about."

"I thought maybe your farmers grew blue roosters?" teased Paul.

Evelyn's background was in architectural history, so she was inspired to share history with Paul. Next, she introduced him to the architecture of the Guthrie Theater.

The theater was closed so they drove around to see the "endless bridge" which overlooked the Mississippi River.

"We have a vibrant theater community here in the Twin Cities," she said, all the while hoping at some point, he would escort her to a production.

"But if you're not into theater we have Target Field where the Minnesota Twins play all summer long." She wasn't much into sports, but she wanted to keep her options open.

By this time, they were hungry, and she headed for the French Meadow Café for lunch. After soup and a sandwich, they shared a slice of decadent triple chocolate mousse cake. That's when she realized he was very fond of desserts.

They returned home exhausted and stuffed.

The day had certainly put a smile on Paul's face, and Evelyn enjoyed the company of this nice-looking young man. Although old enough to be his mother, she enjoyed practicing her flirting skills on him. A trait you probably never outgrow!

The widows were anxious to hear about the "date" with Paul. They were not looking for a male relationship, but he had grabbed their attention.

Edith loved baking, but with her friends always on a diet, she didn't have anyone to bake for. When she learned Paul liked desserts, she dropped off some of her famous homemade cherry pecan cookies along with a smile she didn't often share. That was the beginning of weekly treats waiting for him.

Being a single man, he probably didn't do much cooking. Lillian decided he had to have some of her homemade Minnesota wild rice soup.

The desserts, homemade meals and dinner invitations just kept coming.

Dora took a different approach. She used naivety and every time she saw him, she had a household question for him.

"Paul, could you help me reach a bowl on the top shelf of my cupboard?"

"Could you check and see if my thermostat is working properly?"

"What seems to be wrong with my computer?"

Dora kept Paul busy. And she liked the fact that he could drive at night. He couldn't resist her charms. This older woman was so sweet and innocent, he thought. Although an educated woman and an outspoken member of her book club, throughout her life this helpless façade had been her trademark.

Paul found he had little time to spend in mourning. He was being well cared for.

But all the attention soon got the better of him. He felt overwhelmed with all the nice, kind widows' attentions. He needed some space.

So, when Paul was contacted by a former colleague about a part-time job open in his field, it piqued his interest. He had long-time friends in Chicago. This part-time job there was intriguing.

He didn't let on to the widows that he was thinking about moving back to Chicago.

When he put his condo on the market the ladies were shocked. In the halls and in the garage, word spread that Paul was leaving.

"Oh, Paul, you can't leave. You have become like family to us."

But this didn't stop Paul from forging ahead with his plans to move back to Chicago.

He would miss the ladies, but he often felt like he was living with his mother.

As the last of the household items were loaded onto the moving truck, curtains were pulled aside, and glum faces peered out of the windows. It had been a long time since they remembered being as happy as they had been when Paul lived in the condo. His presence ignited their youthful spirit. Once again, they were suffering a loss: a loss of a friend, a loss of a spring in their step and a wakeup call into their mortality.

The moving truck pulled away. Paul honked, rolled his car window down and waved goodbye to the Widows of Woodhill.

That afternoon Evelyn was out for her afternoon walk with her friend Hazel. Hazel spotted something shiny laying on the asphalt of the Woodhill parking lot.

"What is that?"

Evelyn picked it up and was shocked to recognize it as the diamond and ruby butterfly brooch that was passed on to her from her grandmother. *What was it doing here?*

Evelyn racked her brain to figure out how it could have gotten from her jewelry case to the parking lot. The last thing she remembered was Paul's car parked there before he left.

Word spread quickly about the lost and found brooch. The ladies decided to check their closets to make sure their treasures were safe.

Meredith had a prized collection of antique perfume bottles that were neatly displayed on three walls of her office. She had collected them for years. Those with

Victorian glass, unique shapes or in sterling silver or hand-blown glass bottles were the most valuable. Her most cherished bottles were missing from her collection.

Edith loved to read and had collected several first edition books. Absent from her collection were the most valuable titles.

Paul had spent a lot of time fixing things in Dora's unit. Her husband was a coin collector and had an assortment of rare coins. His whole collection was missing.

This was not a coincidence— all these missing valuables. It wasn't long before they put their heads together and realized the common denominator was Paul.

They reported the stolen items to the police but the prognosis for finding these items was not hopeful. Both the Minneapolis and Chicago police could not find an address under Paul's name living in either city. They suspected it was an alias.

To this day the Widows of Woodhill wonder how this could have happened. Paul was such a charming man.

 Kathryn M. Holmes has published four books, *I Stand with Courage: One Woman's Journey to Conquer Paralysis,* the story of her recovery from a below the waist paralysis. *Reflections,* a self-published book providing bits of wisdom and reflection on family, friends, dating, marriage, society, the workplace, grandchildren and aging. *Watershed Moments,* stories from men and women who experienced life challenges. After the death of her husband, she compiled *Thoughts and Prayers for those Experiencing Loss.* These books can be found on Amazon.com. She lives in Minnetonka, Minnesota with her dog, Honey.